Books by Ann Carroll
in the Linford Romance Library:

CHAMPAGNE HARVEST

A PLACE TO BELONG

The illegitimate daughter of a scullery maid, Lily Baines has been brought up by the Westfalls — not quite family, not quite a servant, not quite sure of where she belongs. When she meets the handsome Jude Mitchell, she finds a most alarming attraction flaring within her. Jude, though, is visiting Westfall Manor with a view to courting Prudence, the daughter of the house, and Lily will not endanger her friend's marriage prospects. But he's taken rather a shine to Lily . . .

ANN CARROLL

A PLACE
TO BELONG

Complete and Unabridged

LINFORD
Leicester

First published in Great Britain in 2017

First Linford Edition
published 2018

A catalogue record for this book is available
from the British Library.

ISBN 978–1–4448–3936–4

Published by
F. A. Thorpe (Publishing)
Anstey, Leicestershire

Set by Words & Graphics Ltd.
Anstey, Leicestershire
Printed and bound in Great Britain by
T. J. International Ltd., Padstow, Cornwall

This book is printed on acid-free paper

1

The clattering of horses' hooves shattered the tranquillity of the hot September afternoon. Lily Baines had been picking apples in the Westfalls' orchard. At the sound of the commotion, she dropped the basket, hitched up her skirt and raced towards the bordering hedgerow.

Standing on tiptoe she saw the approaching carriage hurtling towards her. It was pulled by two black horses, and Lily saw at once that they were travelling far too fast for this rutted, pot-holed track. No one in their right mind travelled at such a speed along here.

'Slow down!' she shouted as the horses drew level.

The coachman merely cracked his whip in the air, urging the horses to go faster. For a fleeting second she

1

glimpsed the solitary passenger inside the carriage. He seemed unperturbed at being driven at breakneck speed and Lily wondered if it could be Prudence's suitor. He wasn't due for hours yet, although if he'd travelled all the way to Sussex from London at this rate, it could indeed be him.

She would soon know. There was a fork in the road ahead. If the carriage veered right, then his destination was indeed Westfall Manor. And if that was the case, she needed to hurry back if she was to make apple pie for pudding tonight as promised.

But just as the horses veered to the right, there came the most awful wood-against-metal grinding crunch. The carriage lurched to one side, stopping the horses in their tracks and shooting the coachman clean off his seat to land on the stony ground. A moment later both horses were rearing and whinnying in fright.

For the carriage wheel to get stuck in a rut didn't really come as a shock to

Lily, but nevertheless, she broke into a run. If the driver didn't scramble clear quickly, the horses' hooves could catch him a nasty blow. And if Prudence's suitor *was* the passenger, Lily felt it her duty to make sure he wasn't hurt. It was one thing warning Prudence that her father's old friend, the widower Jude Mitchell, sounded totally unsuitable for an eighteen-year-old; another to render him unsuitable owing to the fact that he was dead.

Finding a gap in the thorny hedgerow, Lily squeezed through, dragging twigs and leaves with her, snagging her clothing on the sharp prickles. As she ran towards the stricken carriage, she saw, to her relief, the passenger emerging from it. Quickly, he set about dragging the coachman to the side of the road, out of danger from flailing hooves. He attempted to calm the frightened horses, but it was clear to Lily that he had little equestrian experience.

Thinking swiftly, she pulled off her

linen shawl as she ran. Reaching the carriage, she thrust the garment at the passenger, aware that if he was Jude Mitchell, he was nothing like she imagined. There was no time to take stock, however. 'Here, cover the horse's eyes. If he can't see, he'll calm down.'

The man turned his head, clearly startled to see her, and to Lily's annoyance he cast a lingering glance over her before looking at the shawl she was offering. Glancing down, she saw to her dismay that her blouse had lost its two top buttons, and there was far too much cleavage on show. She hoped her glare was scathing enough to make him concentrate on calming the horses before they hurt themselves or anyone else.

'I'll give it a try,' he said, taking the square of embroidered linen and, somehow avoiding the thrashing hooves, managing to drape it over the nearest horse's eyes like a headscarf. Miraculously, it did the trick. The horse stopped its frantic rearing and stood calmly, steam rising from its glistening body. The other horse followed suit, and within seconds both were perfectly still.

The passenger looked astonished. 'Well, I'll be damned!'

'I certainly hope not,' said Lily, not caring for his language. It was hardly the sort of vocabulary to use in front of a young lady. She turned away, holding her dishevelled blouse together as she strode over to the coachman, now sitting on a grassy verge getting his breath back. 'I know I should ask if you're hurt, but actually you brought this accident on yourself. Surely you could see that this lane isn't suitable for charging along at breakneck speed!'

The man got to his feet, dusting himself down and rubbing his back. Lily felt instantly sorry for being so unsympathetic. 'It's the first time I've been to this part of Sussex, and my passenger was in a hurry.'

'More haste, less speed!' stated Lily, repeating a phrase often used by the manor's cook, Mrs Pritchard — a woman who seemed to have an appropriate expression for all occasions. 'Well, now you see where such haste has got you!'

Lily spun round to point to the lopsided carriage, only to find that the passenger, whoever he was, was standing so close behind her that she stepped right into him.

The palms of her hands landed flat against his chest. The heat and firmness of his body through his loose-fitting white shirt seemed to burn her, and she sprang backwards as if struck by a flame. 'Oh!'

Her touch didn't seem to have startled him, however. If anything, it seemed to make his eyes smoulder as he gazed down at her. He had eyes the colour of a summer's sky and a face that was lean and angled, strong cheekbones and a jawline that warned of arrogance, yet his mouth seemed on the verge of a smile. There was a small scar over his right eyebrow and his hair was raven black, swept back from his brow and falling in silky strands to his broad shoulders. The entire appearance of the man and his close proximity caused her heart to flutter. It was a sensation quite new — and alarming — to her.

Lily's own violet-coloured eyes swept from that far-too-handsome face to his throat, noticing a tangle of dark hairs through the laced-up slit at the neck of his shirt. His style of garb was quite buccaneer, like the character Don Juan that she'd read about in a novel in Sir Joseph's library. His shirt was tucked into the wide and ornate leather belt of his buttoned-up breeches, and those in turn tucked into knee-high leather boots. His stance was firm, legs a little apart as if he was aboard a ship on the high seas.

Immediately she halted her fanciful thoughts, aware that he was smiling at her. It was far too familiar a smile: certainly not a respectful smile, a downright flirtatious smile — and she tugged her blouse together again, wishing the buttons hadn't pinged off as she'd battled through the hedgerow.

'My dear lady, we are indebted to you. That was an incredibly brave thing to do. You could have been struck by the horses' hooves.'

He had a deep, melodic voice, which Lily was loath to admit sounded like music to her ears. A lock of sleek black hair had flopped untidily over his forehead, and she had an irresistible urge to stretch up on tiptoe and push it back from his eyes. She stiffened her resolve. Quite clearly he knew how handsome he was, and no doubt he thought he could charm every woman he met. Well, it was *not* going to work with her.

Feeling as stiff and starched as one of Lady Hester's gowns, Lily said, 'More to the point is the reckless way the coachman came hurtling along the lane . . . '

'We apologise.' His smile widened, making tiny lines appear around his wickedly sparkling eyes, as if he found this all so amusing. '*I* apologise. The coachman was only following my orders.'

It was as if her body was on fire. Men often smiled and tried to win a smile back from her, and once she'd even had a marriage proposal — of sorts. But never had a man so outrageously handsome paid her such attention. She felt completely out of her depth, and the worst of it was, she found it almost impossible not to be drawn to those seductive eyes and the curve of his lips.

Drawing on all her willpower, Lily tilted her chin, looking beyond him to the stricken carriage. She was not about to stand here arguing all day. She had better things to do. Although, if she was honest, she had very little to do; but that wasn't by choice. She was neither family nor staff at Westfall Manor, merely their guilty burden.

'Being sorry is hardly going to get the carriage out of that pothole. You're going to need help.' As she spoke, she could practically hear Lady Hester's exact tone in her words. No wonder Prudence teased her sometimes for being so prim and proper.

'We certainly will need help,' the passenger mused, striding back to the carriage. He adopted that buccaneer stance once more: legs apart, feet firmly planted on the ground, hands on hips. With his back to her, Lily couldn't fail to notice the width of his shoulders, and how his back tapered down to a lean waist. Her gaze strayed lower, to the snug contours of his buttocks and muscled thighs. She assumed he was in his early thirties, and by his physique he clearly led an active life. But she wondered if his stance and pose were for her benefit. He was probably used to being admired by the opposite sex, and to her shame she realised she had fallen into his trap.

It was impossible not to gaze at the firmness of his athletic body. He was the stuff of her secret fantasies. However, fantasy and daydreaming were the limit of her experience with men. But in her head her thoughts drifted wildly. She felt the sudden rush of colour to her cheeks — just as he turned to speak to her again.

He went to say something, and then stopped. Instead, his lips twitched into a knowing smile. 'You look very pretty when you blush.'

'I'm certainly not blushing,' she snapped, her bosom rising in annoyance at his audacity. 'I'm flustered, and understandably so!' And, marching past him, she retrieved her shawl that was still draped over the horse's head. She was glad to slip it around her shoulders, covering her cleavage, leaving her feeling just a little less vulnerable.

With the horses standing perfectly calmly, she stroked their noses. 'You poor things. What a fright that must have given you. But it's all right now. Good boys.'

'You know about horses?'

He was standing right beside her again, and Lily marvelled at the softness of his step for such a large individual. She was quite tall and willowy herself, standing at five feet six, but he was head and shoulders taller than her.

She flashed a look at him from beneath her eyelashes. 'I know that they react to kindness rather than a whip.'

'I don't whip them, miss,' the coachman interrupted, coming over and fussing his steeds. 'These are my babies, they're everything to me. I wouldn't treat them badly. The whip's just for the sound, and they love to run, honestly. Just bad luck that we hit a pothole.'

Judging by the way the horses were nuzzling his chest and hand, Lily sensed he was telling the truth. But she kept her tone clipped and her delicate chin tilted. 'I'm pleased to hear that. Only now we need to get some help.'

The buccaneer passenger turned at the word *we*, and she instantly regretted including herself in the suggestion. And why, oh why, did he have to keep looking at her in such a disarming way? He really was quite the expert in flirtation.

'I noticed that we passed through a village a mile or so back,' the passenger said, the intimacy of his gaze causing her stomach to flutter and her heartbeat to quicken. 'Could anyone there assist us, do you think?'

'Possibly,' Lily answered, thinking of the blacksmith or Ted Draper, one of the farmers off the estate — who had proposed to her not six months ago. She quickly decided that the village blacksmith would be their best choice. Ted Draper was a good man, and would certainly help anyone, but his proposal — so out of the blue — had left her feeling awkward around him. 'Fortunately, there's a blacksmith in the village who owns a very sturdy Shire horse. This won't be the first time he's come to the aid of reckless travellers.'

The buccaneer passenger, whoever he was, didn't seem perturbed at being labelled *reckless*. Rather, his face lit up as he turned to the coachman. 'Excellent! So, my good man, you stay with the horses and my luggage, while the young lady and I find a kindly Samaritan to help us out of our predicament.'

'Right you are, sir.'

Lily's eyes widened in alarm. She had no intention of going anywhere with this man, this stranger. The prospect sent tremors through her slender body. Heatedly, she said, 'I'm sure you'll find him perfectly easily enough. His is the first cottage on the right, opposite the duck pond. He has a painted sign on his gate saying 'Carter and Son, Blacksmith'.'

His far-too-handsome head tilted to one side, clear blue eyes appealing to her better nature. 'Am I right in thinking that you know the blacksmith, and he knows you?'

This man had a charm that did the strangest thing to her common sense. 'Well, yes, but . . . '

'Then we may have more luck in

14

enlisting his help if you were to accompany me.'

She looked at the hopeful, boyish, irresistible expression on his face, and felt all resistance melt away. That look had no doubt charmed many a young lady to act against her better judgement, and it thoroughly irritated her to realise she was fighting a losing battle too.

But she had an apple pie to make. She'd promised Mrs Pritchard the cook. She wrestled with her conscience, and the fact that it was dangerous and irresponsible to go walking through quiet country lanes with a stranger — a very disarming, exceedingly handsome stranger at that.

As if reading her mind, he stepped back and bowed outrageously. 'Forgive me, I'm being presumptuous. Your kindness has exceeded all expectations already. I'm sorry for laying our troubles on your shoulders.' That expression was back. Intense blue eyes lingered on her mouth, making her feel that he longed to kiss her. 'And very attractive shoulders too, if I may say so.'

Heat rushed up her throat and into her cheeks again. He was an out-and-out flirt, a womaniser. No doubt Prudence would know how to deal with such a man: she was an outrageous flirt herself. But Lily had no idea how to handle him. She'd never been in a situation where a man was so clearly attempting to seduce her.

'You may *not* say so!' She lifted her chin, blushing or not, and met that gaze with a hostile glare of her own. 'And I find your attentions and attitude quite . . . unacceptable.'

She had the feeling that the coachman was hiding a smirk, and no doubt the passenger found this whole situation titillating.

His expression became suddenly quite forlorn, however. 'I apologise profusely. And, while I have no right to ask any favours of you, your continued assistance would be greatly valued.'

He looked so humble suddenly that

Lily felt the urge to giggle. She rallied quickly; she had no intention of dropping her guard where this man was concerned.

Nevertheless, the carriage needed to be moved. The Westfalls' guest — if this wasn't him — was due within the next few hours. She certainly hoped this man was not Jude Mitchell. This individual was clearly not a suitable husband for her dear friend Prudence — nor, in fact, for any woman in her right mind. A man about to meet his possible new wife should not be flirting with the first woman he bumped into.

Making her decision, and aware that she sounded like a prim schoolmistress, she marched off towards the village, calling back over her shoulder, 'Very well, I'll introduce you to Abe Carter. He'll want paying, you know!'

He caught up with her in a few easy strides and she sensed his bemusement. She focused straight ahead, on the leafy green lane bordered by hedgerows lush with plump blackberries. The air was sweet with the fragrance of ripe fruit and wild flowers. But Lily was more aware — acutely aware of the man at her side, tall and powerful, his gait lithe; limbs fluid and graceful in a fearsomely masculine way. And the breathlessness she felt as she walked on was not due to any lack of fitness on her part. It was because of him. Her body felt aflame and there was a tingling of desire deep inside her abdomen. She tried to banish the sensation, to think of other things; anything to take her mind off this undeniably attractive — if annoying — man at her side.

Deliberately, she concentrated her thoughts on the morning's events, when she had been summoned into the Westfalls' drawing room. They had all been lined up, Sir Joseph, Lady Hester and Prudence, overshadowed by sombre oil paintings of past occupiers of the Westfalls' Sussex estate. The only cheerful face had been Prudence's. As Lily had approached them, smart in her long apple-green skirt and ruffled buttoned-up blouse, her honey-coloured hair fastened neatly in a twist at the back of her neck, she saw Sir Joseph catch his breath. Immediately, his wife had cast him a sharp, reproachful glance.

The moment passed fleetingly, and while Lily wondered what had caused their reactions she hadn't ventured to ask. She had simply bobbed a little curtsey, as if she were a member of staff, and politely said good morning to them all.

'Good morning, Lily,' they had replied in unison, and then Prudence had lunged forwards and hugged her.

'Happy eighteenth birthday, Lily! You've caught me up! Oh, how I wish it was *my* birthday, getting presents. Lucky, lucky you!'

'I know,' Lily had agreed, and would loved to have matched her enthusiasm had Lady Hester's gaze not been quite so severe.

Prudence linked her arm through her

father's. He patted her hand affection-ately, but his blue-grey eyes were still focused on Lily, oblivious to his wife's dagger-like glances. His expression was curious, as if he couldn't quite believe what he was seeing.

Usually he avoided eye contact. Over the years he had averted his gaze so often that Lily had given up hoping he would show her any real affection. Not that she really expected any, not any more. They had given her a good education and a good home, but she was well aware that her presence here was not out of love. It was an act of charity — which Hester regularly reminded her of.

Lily's foot suddenly caught in a pothole and she stumbled. Jolted back to reality, she felt a strong arm around her waist, catching her and stopping her from falling headlong into the rutted lane.

'Careful!' came that deep melodic voice.

Glad not to have gone sprawling into

the dust, Lily realised he was in no hurry to release her. And, to her shame, she was in no hurry to be released. The strength of his arm was reassuring and his touch was sending delicious shivers up and down her spine. She had never been held so tightly nor so closely. Her cheeks flamed again and reluctantly she wriggled from his grip, putting an end to this foolishness at once.

No doubt he was in the habit of catching women as they stumbled. She wouldn't put it past him to have tripped her just so he could catch her.

'Thank you!' she said stiffly. 'This lane really is dreadful.'

'You were miles away. What were you thinking?'

She looked up from beneath her long sweep of eyelashes. 'If you must know, I was thinking what a fine birthday this was turning out to be!'

His black eyebrows arched in surprise. 'It's your birthday? Well, may I offer you the warmest of good wishes!' And, to her astonishment, he took her hand and brought it up to his lips.

It happened so smoothly and so suddenly that Lily could only hold her breath as he softly placed a kiss on the back of her hand. In doing so, his intense blue eyes locked on to hers, smouldering with a desire that sent shivers darting through her loins.

She drew her hand swiftly away, annoyed by her own emotions as much as his audacity. He was certainly a womaniser, a man out to charm every female he met. And while the prospect of him kissing parts of her anatomy other than her hand made her feel quite weak at the knees, she wasn't in the habit of succumbing to such blatant seduction. The fact was, she had never even kissed a man, let alone anything else. And she would certainly not be giving her innocence away to the likes of this individual.

'I apologise again,' he said, not looking in the least apologetic. 'I don't even know your name.'

'Nor are you likely to!' Lily answered

abruptly, deciding he was far too forward. 'Why should I give you my name when I don't know the first thing about you?'

Nothing she said seemed to affect his good humour. He simply smiled as if he sensed her pompous demeanour was just an act, then bowed in a ridiculously flamboyant manner and said, 'My beautiful lady, allow me to introduce myself. Jude Mitchell, merchant fleet owner and captain, at your service.'

2

Lily wasn't really surprised to discover he was Prudence's suitor, but she was disappointed — bitterly disappointed. Her dear friend's potential fiancé was a flirt and a womaniser. As predicted, she was quite correct in guessing Sir Joseph's old friend would not be suitable for Prudence, but not because he was too old or too dreary — far from it. He was far too experienced and too flirtatious to be faithful to Prudence or anyone. Here he was, travelling all the way from London to meet Prudence with a view to marriage, and he was instantly trying to charm *her* into bed.

She concentrated hard on these facts and pushed aside the realisation that, to her shame, she was physically attracted to Prudence's prospective husband. And Prudence was her dearest friend. Not a sister, but the closest she would ever come to having family.

'I see,' she murmured as she walked on, taking care to avoid the ruts and potholes.

He strode along beside her. 'Now that you know I'm not some wanted criminal, will you tell me your name? And where you are from? I glimpsed you in that orchard. Your home must be nearby?'

'It is, actually!' she declared, guessing he was going to be utterly ashamed of his flirtatious behaviour when he discovered she was one of the Westfall . . . no, not family; not even staff. But she did live at Westfall Manor. And she knew his reason for calling. She stopped abruptly and tilted her chin at him, looking him straight in the eye. 'That was the Westfalls' orchard, and all the farms and cottages around here are part of the Westfall estate . . . '

'And you are Prudence Westfall, Sir Joseph's daughter!' His face lit up. 'Yes, I can see you are. I remember when I was a boy, and he visited my father at

London Docks, he had golden hair, exactly your shade. I know his locks are quite silver these days . . . '

Lily finally squeezed a word in edgeways. 'No, I am not Prudence, and I'm not Sir Joseph's daughter.'

He looked stunned. As if he was never wrong. For the first time since meeting him, Lily saw that he was quite thrown by her words. Good! He was far too arrogant, confident and conceited. He needed to be knocked off his perch.

A frown creased his broad, tanned forehead. 'You're his niece, then?'

'We are no relation. I live at the manor and my name is Lily Baines.'

'Lily Baines!' He seemed to let the words roll over his tongue. 'Then I apologise for my assumptions and I am delighted to make your acquaintance, Lily.'

'Likewise,' she said, because it was the polite thing to say. The Westfalls had brought her up to be well-mannered whatever the circumstances. They'd given her the same nanny and private

26

tutoring as they'd given their only daughter. It was only the hugs and affection that had not been forthcoming.

Sometimes it felt like Sir Joseph and Lady Hester saw her as their cross to bear. Clearly they felt guilty for her growing up as an orphan. Lily knew she was a constant reminder of how they'd failed to notice that their scullery maid, Lillian Baines, was pregnant; failed to notice that eighteen years ago Lillian had gone into labour without a midwife or doctor present. No doubt they constantly rebuked themselves for not doing enough to save Lillian's life, although the baby — Lily — had been born safely.

He touched her arm, which sent unwelcome tingles through her body. She saw that he was merely indicating another pothole ahead that needed avoiding. 'So, Lily, what do you do at the manor?'

She hesitated. Sir Joseph and Hester asked nothing from her. She wasn't even expected to work as one of the staff. She wished she *was* a member of staff. At least then she would know her place. Know what her role in life was. But she couldn't explain all that to him. Instead, she said, 'I cook,' which was the truth. 'I'm not the main cook. I'm more of an apprentice.'

'Excellent. They say the way to a man's heart is through his stomach.' There was amusement in his voice and Lily felt his gaze burning through her. Deliberately, she focused straight ahead.

'Mrs Pritchard, the cook at the manor, is always saying the same; but believe me, Mr Mitchell . . . ' She turned to look up into his face, to stress the point. ' . . . I have no intentions of worming my way into anyone's heart. I cook because I enjoy cooking, and of course to feed people.'

'Admirable!' His white teeth glinted in the afternoon sunshine. 'And will I be tasting any of your no doubt delicious culinary delights?'

'You *were* to have apple pie and custard for your pudding this evening. That's what I was doing in the orchard. Now, however, other things seem to have taken priority.'

'Alas, that's true. And I've no one to blame but myself.' He smiled ruefully. 'It's a pity you have to work on your birthday.'

She almost said that she didn't *have* to work. It was her choice. But she couldn't explain that to him, so she replied, 'I love cooking. I don't think of it as a chore.'

'Will you be celebrating with your family later?'

Lily's eyes fluttered shut for a second. Birthdays had never been a reason for celebration. How could she celebrate the day her mother died? She prayed her chin didn't quiver nor her voice catch in her throat as she said, 'I don't have any family.'

His stride faltered. 'Your parents are dead? I'm sorry to hear that.'

A wave of sorrow rushed up from

29

inside her, overwhelming her. Her mother had been just her age when she died. Sir Joseph and Lady Hester had told her very little about her mother, their scullery maid. What she knew of her had come from Mrs Pritchard. Controlling her voice, hoping desperately to hide any tremors, she answered, 'Thank you.'

A firm hand gripped her elbow. She assumed it was to warn her of another pothole, but his expression was sympathetic, his blue eyes shining, as if he knew what she was feeling. Lily remembered then that he was a widower. His grief could be worse, as he had known his wife, whereas she had never known her mother. And as for her father, she had no idea at all.

'What happened?' he asked, his tone far gentler than she'd expect from a man like him.

But she wasn't about to tell him that she was the Westfall family's guilty secret. That she was illegitimate. He would naturally think badly of her mother. So she simply replied, 'It was a long time ago, I don't remember very much, and I don't care to talk about it.' She cast him a quick glance, wondering if she were being impolite. He was only being concerned. 'I apologise if that seems a little abrupt.'

'I'm the one who's sorry,' he said, his voice quite sombre now. 'Sorry for your loss. I know how that feels.'

He fell silent and remained silent, lost in thought as they walked into the village. The only sounds now were birdsong, the occasional flapping of a wood pigeon's wings as it took flight, and the clicking of Jude Mitchell's leather boots on the sun-baked road.

Occasionally, Lily glanced at him, glimpsed that chiselled profile. His features seemed set in stone now, and she almost regretted the fact that the flirtatious, smiling Jude Mitchell had vanished. And she had no idea how to bring him back.

Perhaps Prudence would be good for him after all. Despite being almost the same age and having grown up together, she and Prudence were so very different. Prudence was like a pretty china doll, while she was like a willowy leaf blown in from the garden. Lily's complexion was fresh and pale — when she wasn't blushing — while Prudence deliberately added rouge and powder. Lily was slender while Prudence was curvaceous, although Lily imagined that she might also look so voluptuous if she laced her corset as tightly and wore such low-cut necklines. But that wasn't her style, and she certainly couldn't flaunt her charms as shamelessly as Prudence did and get away with it.

Then there were hairstyles. Prudence liked her long black hair to be curled or in ringlets, which Lily enjoyed styling for her. But for herself, she preferred her honey-coloured long hair to be loose and free, or else neatly pinned up in a twist at the back of her head. It was obvious that Prudence got her dark locks and blue eyes from

Hester, although the older woman's gaze was cold and lacked sparkle. Whereas Lily was forced to admit that she had no idea whether it was her mother or her father whom she'd inherited her golden hair and almond-shaped violet-coloured eyes from.

Prudence was the apple of her parents' eye, and understandably so. She was as pretty as a picture with her dimpled cheeks and mischievous eyes. But her head was crammed full of the latest fashions, or thoughts of which eligible bachelor would be next to try and win her hand in matrimony. The latest one being Jude Mitchell.

Lily cast a sidelong glance at Jude, and knew without a shadow of doubt that Prudence would be smitten by him, particularly when he turned on his charm. And he, when he set those roving eyes on Prudence, would be equally as enraptured. How could any man not be?

For some unknown reason, the thought sent her heart plummeting.

★ ★ ★

Lily Baines! Jude let the name resound in his head as he walked beside her towards the village. Lily! The name suited her. She was as slender and elegant as a lily, and as beautiful. And no doubt, if she dropped the angry façade, she would be as sweet.

He sensed that she wasn't the shrew that she pretended to be — and how he would love to break through that outer shell that kept him at his distance!

But the most stunning thing about Lily Baines was that for the first time since Isabella passed away five years ago, he felt alive again. Felt a reason to smile again. And he had to admit he'd been a grinning fool ever since setting eyes on Lily. But he couldn't help it. There was something about Lily that touched him, and apple pie or no apple pie, she had somehow found a place in his heart.

There was an immediate problem, however. For one thing, he had no idea whether she was already married or betrothed — plus the fact that she clearly didn't like him. Yes, that was a major problem. But also, he was here to meet Prudence. How strange that he'd mistaken Lily for Sir Joseph's daughter. It wasn't just the hair colour; there was more to it than that. Ah, well! Perhaps when he saw Prudence he would realise that Lily actually had very little resemblance to the Westfall family. Perhaps it was just wishful thinking that Lily was the daughter he had come to meet.

He tried to concentrate on his decision to meet Prudence but realised that she was going to have to be very special indeed to impress him after meeting Lily. Damn it! She was back in his thoughts. What the hell was the matter with him? Could he no longer string two thoughts together without Lily Baines being a part of them?

Prudence. Prudence Westfall. How did Prudence Mitchell sound? Odd, that was how it sounded. But Lily

Mitchell . . . A warm feeling spread through his chest. *Lily Mitchell*. He liked the sound of that.

But the most unbelievable, incredible thing was that from somewhere deep inside he felt the stirrings of hope. When Isabella had died of pneumonia, all hope, happiness and even the reason to live, had died with her.

He'd had to keep going. He had his father's merchant ships to run, which the men depended upon. So he had ploughed every last drop of energy into his fleet. He had joined the men on voyages around Europe — only to return home to an empty bed.

Loneliness and the lack of conversation had gradually made him consider looking for a wife — certainly not someone to love. Isabella had been his one true love. He couldn't hope to find another woman to love and be loved back. He'd been fortunate to have had that once in his life. He couldn't expect it a second time.

But to have a female companion, a

friend who was pleasing to the eye rather than the rough-necked crewmen he was forced to look at day in, day out ... And if their friendship developed into a sexual union too, then he would be complete. There was no denying the heartbreaking void in his life since losing his wife.

He glanced at Lily marching along beside him. The thought of taking her to his bed sent his blood racing, and deep inside him that spark of desire reignited and began to flare.

3

Reaching the outskirts of the village, Lily, without thinking, touched Jude's arm to point ahead towards a white-walled thatched cottage. Beneath her hand she felt the tightening of sinew in his forearm, and before she could draw back, his hand covered hers and he inclined his head a little to catch what she was about to say.

'Abe Carter's cottage,' Lily said, pulling free from his hold. 'And look, there's his Shire horse. Isn't he magnificent?' She didn't wait for a response but, hitching up her skirt, ran on ahead up the lane.

The horse was grazing in the field attached to the blacksmith's cottage. He was a huge, sturdy, dark brown creature with a white streak down his nose and a black tail and mane. Reaching the fence, Lily plucked a handful of lush grass, climbed onto the bottom wooden slat and held out the grass for the horse. He needed little encouragement and came plodding purposefully towards her, tail swishing and mighty head nodding.

The horse was chomping on the fresh grass when Jude sauntered over and stood next to her. She tried hard not to look at him, but it was impossible. And because she was standing on the wooden slat she was eye to eye with him. For the briefest of moments their gazes locked. His were the most beautiful eyes she had ever seen in a man — not that she was used to gazing so intimately into a man's face. They were the deepest vivid blue, the whites clear as snow, framed within thick black lashes. She tore her gaze away, hoping not to blush again. 'Isn't he the most beautiful creature you have ever seen?'

'Not quite,' he murmured, and when she cast him a puzzled glance saw that he was still looking at her.

So he was still flirting. Despite him

being aware that she lived at the manor and would know his purpose for visiting. Obviously he thought it acceptable to come a-wooing one woman, and to lavish compliments and lingering looks on another.

Prudence needed to know what sort of man he was. Marriage was about forsaking all others, wasn't it? Well, clearly he wasn't to be trusted anywhere near a woman without trying to flirt with her.

Lily's attention switched to Abe Carter working in the yard. He was as broad as he was tall, a giant of a man with biceps like ripe pumpkins and not a hair on his head. He was bare-chested, bronzed skin glistening with sweat, hammering a metal rim to a barrel. The sound of metal clanging against metal rang out across the field.

'He looks capable of hauling the carriage out without the aid of a horse.'

Lily stifled a laugh. He was right, but she had no intention of gracing his comments with a smile of approval.

Stiffly, she replied, 'Indeed.'

'Shall we go around and talk to him?' Jude reached for her hand as she stepped down from the fence.

To ignore it would have been churlish, and so she allowed her hand to be encircled by his. 'Thank you,' she murmured with an air of primness.

He adopted a similar manner. 'My pleasure.'

She had the feeling that he was teasing, but not sure how to react, she marched on around the perimeter of the field and into the blacksmith's cobbled yard. An open fire blazed inside a bricked fireplace. The heat quite took her aback. Abe finished hammering the rim around the barrel, wiped his face with a rag, and ambled over to them.

'Afternoon, Miss Lily,' said Abe, looking from her to Jude. 'Afternoon, sir. And what can I be doing for you folk?'

Jude stepped forward: they were equal in height, but Abe seemed twice the girth. 'I am fervently hoping that I can enlist your help,' began Jude, going on to explain the situation and waxing lyrical over Lily coming to their rescue, saving him and the carriage driver from serious injury.

Lily realised he was being deliberately overdramatic, but Abe Carter appeared to enjoy the story and warmed to Jude's good humour.

Abe finally nodded his sweat-glistening head. 'It was your good fortune that Miss Lily was there then, Sir.'

Jude turned and smiled directly into her eyes. The effect sent unexpected tingles running through her abdomen. 'Indeed it was, Mr Carter. Indeed it was.'

'I'll get a few things together, and put a halter on Thunder. He'll be glad of a walk out.'

Jude thanked him with the promise of paying him well for his work. 'While you're getting ready, we'll wait beside the pond. I think we need to get into the shade for a while.' He raised one dark eyebrow at Lily, intimating that she might like to join him. He extended an arm towards the willow tree as if he were inviting her into his boudoir. 'Shall we?'

The huge weeping willow tree draping its branches into the duck pond looked wonderfully shady, though a little too intimate and secluded for her liking. But it was a hot afternoon, and the longer she spent in Jude Mitchell's company, the more hot and bothered she was becoming.

Lily crossed the lane, feeling as if she were indeed stepping into his private sanctum. Heatedly, she reminded herself that this really wasn't in keeping with her position. This was Prudence's suitor: intimate moments like this were not meant for her. Yet she continued walking towards the big old willow tree as if she had quite lost the will to make her own decisions. But it was a delightful tree. Weeping willows were her favourite, and she had actually sketched this one on many occasions — never, however, with a man at her side, a man such as Jude Mitchell, watching her every move and gesture.

The willow's long trailing fronds splayed out, encircling the gnarled old trunk. Jude stepped through first, holding the cascade of greenery aside for her to walk beneath, as if he were holding back a curtain. As he let it fall, she felt as if every nerve ending was on fire. They could barely be seen under here. It was cool and shady and exciting.

The close proximity of Jude sent her pulse racing; needing to get herself under control, she decided the best plan was to talk — and keep talking until Abe Carter joined them.

'I've sketched this tree many times,' Lily began, concentrating on the rough bark as if it were the most fascinating thing in the world. 'But always from the outside, never from its heart.'

'You draw? I admire anyone with such skills. Sadly, I neither draw nor paint, but I do write sonnets and even sing on occasions.'

She gaped at him. 'You sing?'

'There are times when you're at sea that you need to keep up the crew's spirits, and warbling out an old sea shanty or two helps pass the time.' To her surprise, he put one hand on his chest made a wide sweeping gesture with the other, beginning to sing in a voice that was rich and melodious.

Lily listened, captivated. Wishing that he had a warbling, cracked voice, or sang out of key or like a frog. But his tone was perfection. Clearly he had a good ear for music. Lady Hester and Prudence were both accomplished pianists, and Prudence had a lovely singing voice. The knowledge that Jude and Prudence would have music in common ought to have pleased her. The fact that it didn't made her feel quite out of sorts.

When he had finished, she applauded lightly. 'You have a fine voice, Mr Mitchell. I'm sure your ship's crew appreciate your shanties.'

'Perhaps,' he said, for once avoiding her gaze, as if embarrassed by bursting into song. 'Tell me about your drawings. Do you paint also?'

'I dabble,' she said modestly, stroking her hand over the twisted and creviced bark of the tree. 'If I had my sketchpad and paints with me now, I would be tempted to paint this tree with its lovely tangled roots, but I think I would want to include some fairies and elves. It looks like a fairytale tree, don't you think . . . ' Her voice trailed away. He was gazing at her now with a bemused expression on his face.

'You have an enchanting smile, Lily. Has anyone ever told you that?'

His words stunned her. She wasn't used to compliments, and hadn't the faintest idea how to respond. If she were Prudence, she would probably just smile in acknowledgement and accept the fact. But she wasn't Prudence; she lacked her self-confidence. His words left her tongue-tied and feeling foolish.

Fancy babbling on about fantasy woodland creatures to a man such as him, a man whose life was spent on perilous high seas, every day no doubt fraught with danger.

He tilted his head, a softness in his eyes and in the curve to his lips. 'I'm sorry, Lily. I didn't mean to embarrass you.'

'You haven't.' She shrugged, turning heatedly away to concentrate on a family of coots scuttling about on the water, weaving in and out of the trailing branches. 'I embarrass myself, talking about fairies and such whimsical things.'

He closed the space between them. Without raising her eyes she sensed his nearness and her body prickled. 'Not at all. I think the notion is delightful. In fact I think you are de — -'

'All set, sir!' Abe Carter shouted from the lane.

Lily caught the look on Jude Mitchell's face. It was without doubt an amorous look. This man was out to seduce her. That was blatantly obvious. She breathed a sigh of relief that Abe Carter had interrupted them. Undoubtedly this man knew the effect he was having upon her. She was out of her depth here. He was too worldly-wise, too experienced with the opposite sex, and far too attractive. He probably thought she was easy meat.

Despite the fluttering in her abdomen, and the treacherous desire to actually know what his kiss would feel like on parts of her body other than her hand, she wasn't about to become another notch on his belt. She just hoped that she could stop Prudence from becoming one also. Or, worse — stop her from falling into a marriage with a man who clearly could not be trusted.

Hitching up the hem of her skirt, Lily ducked between the willow's cascading branches into the sunlight again. She hurried towards Abe and his horse, feeling as if she had been saved just in the nick of time. Saved from herself

— from doing something very foolish and regrettable.

The sound of Thunder's hooves clip-clopping along the lane as they headed back towards the stricken carriage made a welcome distraction. Lily walked on the right of the Shire horse. There was a solid reliability to his heavy plod. She liked his calming manner. It helped her pounding heartbeat to slow to a more normal rhythm.

Abe Carter walked on the left of the horse, holding the bridle. Not that Thunder was likely to do anything untoward. He seemed in tune with Abe and content to do his bidding. He wore a large collar with chains and brass buckles that rested over his mighty flanks. Jude Mitchell walked alongside Abe, the two chatting like old friends. Lily marvelled at the way Jude seemed able to engage with people so easily. Abe Carter had certainly warmed to him. But it wasn't long before Jude drew her into the conversation. He leant forward to catch sight of her on the other side of the horse.

'You seem to have a way with horses, Lily. Do you ride?'

'Heavens, no! I just think they are the most beautiful of animals. I sketch them. I drew a picture of Thunder once, do you remember, Abe? I think I was about twelve.'

'I remember,' said Abe with a deep chuckle. 'You were such a shy little thing. I'd noticed you sitting on the fence, with your sketch book. Then you came over, thrust the picture at me, and ran like the wind.'

Lily recalled how frightened she'd been of this gigantic man. But she'd decided the portrait of Thunder ought to be his. She smiled at the memory. 'I was a little bit scared of you at the time.'

'I framed that picture, Miss Lily,' he added, startling her. 'And it still has pride of place over my fireplace.'

The news thrilled her beyond belief. 'My goodness! Really?'

'It's a beautiful picture,' said Abe.

'Looks just like him.'

Jude caught her eye again. 'I should love to see your work, Lily.'

She gave a little laugh. 'I think Abe is just being kind. My artwork is not so very special.'

'You're too modest, Miss Lily.'

Needing to draw the attention away from herself, Lily asked, 'Do you ride, Mr Mitchell?'

'Call me Jude; and no, sadly I've never had the opportunity. My wife . . . my late wife, Isabella, used to ride before she met me. It was something we talked about doing together, only . . . '

Lily heard the catch in his voice and wondered what had happened to her — Isabella. She was suddenly wildly curious to know more about Jude Mitchell's life.

Abe brought Thunder to a halt. 'You're welcome to ride on Thunder's back. You both are.'

Lily gasped in surprise. All thoughts of Jude Mitchell's private life vanished at the prospect of riding on Thunder. It

51

had long been a secret desire to ride a horse, but she had never before been offered the opportunity. It was impossible to hide her excitement. However, she declined the offer. 'Thank you, Abe, but I haven't the faintest idea how to ride a horse!'

Jude stroked the Shire horse's mighty head and looked at Lily, his blue eyes glinting with devilment. 'What an opportunity! Your first ride on a horse — and on your birthday! A treat not to be missed!'

Quite taken aback, Lily looked at the eager faces of both Jude Mitchell and Abe Carter. And then she looked at the horse. Her head didn't even come up to his glossy shoulders. Mounting him would be an impossibility — besides, he didn't have a saddle. Nevertheless, a little gurgle of laughter escaped her lips. 'I'd never get up there! And if I did, I'd be afraid I'd fall off.'

'Allow me, Lily,' Jude said, impetuously going down on one knee. He cupped his hands and looked up into her astonished face. 'Hold onto my shoulders and put your right foot into my hands. I'll lift you.'

'I couldn't possibly!' Lily exclaimed, shocked and suddenly breathless at the prospect of making such a spectacle of herself. But yet, the thought of riding on Thunder's back was thrilling. The hesitation must have shown in her face, because Jude wasn't taking no for an answer. He remained on one knee with his hands clasped together, his blue eyes glinting up at her — daring her.

Whether it was the look on his face or the thrill of actually getting on a horse, Lily wasn't sure. But she stepped towards him, trying not to look too excited. 'Oh dear! I'm sure I'll regret this! So tell me again, Mr Mitchell, what do I do?'

'Place both hands on my shoulders, and hold me tightly,' said Jude, settling himself. 'Then place your right foot into my hands. Don't be afraid, now, I won't let you fall.'

'I warn you, I'm very heavy,' Lily

remarked, throwing caution to the wind and doing what he suggested.

She had never, ever in her life placed her hands on a man's shoulders. The sensation sent ripples of pleasure through her body. His shoulders were so broad and her hands seemed so delicate against the expanse of white linen shirt. The heat from his body scorched her palms, and she was utterly aware of how close her body, her breasts, were to his upturned face. Warily, she put her foot into his cupped hands.

'Hold me tight now, Lily!'

He stood slowly, and she felt the flexing of powerful muscles as he straightened his legs and his back, lifting her up into the air as if she weighed no more than a porcelain doll.

'Oh! My goodness!' She gripped his shoulders so tightly, she wondered if her nails were digging into his skin.

In no time she was eye-level with Thunder's broad back. Jude instructed her to sit side-saddle on the horse, even though there was no saddle. Below her, Abe stood holding the bridle, poised ready to catch her should she fall off the other side.

'Hold on to Thunder's collar, Miss Lily,' said Abe, tapping the large contraption that hung around the horse's powerful neck.

Lily did as she was told, but felt none too safe, and was sure that once Thunder began to walk she would tumble off backwards. She guessed she would feel less unstable if she could sit astride the beast. But that would be totally unladylike. 'There is clearly a skill to this, which unfortunately I don't seem to possess. I think I need to get off before I fall off!'

'Sir?' Abe said, as Lily clung on tightly to the collar.

'Don't move, Lily,' said Jude, dashing around to Abe's side of the horse.

In a flash, Abe had cupped his hands just as Jude had, and hoisted him up onto the horse behind her. His powerful legs went astride the horse — and her, holding her securely between his thighs, his arms encircling her to take up the reins, his firm torso pressed against her spine.

Her breath caught in her throat. Never in her life had she experienced such intimacy. She had been brought up living a life that lacked physical closeness. Lady Hester and Sir Joseph had no reason to give her affection. Mrs Pritchard, the closest she had to a mother figure, was kind but brusque and stood no nonsense. And so to feel such closeness from a man — a man such as the far-too-attractive and seductive Jude Mitchell — was more than she could cope with. Her heartbeat raced and shivers of delight shot through her abdomen. Somehow, she kept her composure, despite the tingles and ripples of pleasure darting through every nerve in her body.

A moment later Thunder set off at a slow plod. The sway of the huge animal caused Lily to cry out in alarm. Instantly, Jude adjusted his position, holding the reins in one hand, leaving his left arm to slip around her waist and hold her even more tightly to him. Lily's fear of falling off vanished. But a wave of emotion of a far more intimate type raged through her, sending her heart fluttering so frantically against her ribcage that she was certain Jude Mitchell would be able to feel it.

His lips were perilously close to her ear, his warm breath on her throat. 'How does this feel, Lily?' he murmured.

It felt thrilling and shocking, and like nothing she had experienced in her whole life. The pleasure of being cocooned within his embrace was overwhelming. And at that moment she knew without a shadow of doubt that she would happily reside here in his arms for evermore.

But her throat tightened. She would certainly not be telling him that, however. And she only hoped that the compliant manner in which her body melted against his would not give away her true feelings.

To her relief, he added more clarity to his question. 'Riding a horse for the first time?'

'It . . . it's quite an experience!'

As they ambled on, Lily did her best to ignore the sensation of being held in such an embrace, to ignore the sensual desires sparking within her. His arm around her waist held her possessively, and she wondered recklessly what it would feel like if those strong fingers were to begin stroking her midriff, to touch her breast. Unable to clutch her shawl, she was acutely aware of the way her blouse gaped open in the breeze. She wondered if he was peering over her shoulder to catch a glimpse. Rather than this annoying her, she suddenly wanted his attentions, wanted his touch, wanted more than just his warm breath on her neck. She wanted his lips.

Shocked by these awakening feelings, Lily forced her fanciful thoughts to stop. Determinedly she forced herself to concentrate on the thrill of actually riding a horse rather than the thrill of being held so tightly by Jude Mitchell. She took in the view of the countryside from up here on Thunder's back. The world suddenly looked so very different from this height. She could see over the hedgerows, she could see the sheep in the fields, see birds' nests in the branches. And to be carried along on such a powerful animal's back was beyond words.

She turned her head slightly to glance back at Jude, to see if he was enjoying the view as much as her. But she found him looking at her rather than the scenery. She couldn't help but smile and be honest with him. 'Do you know what, Mr Mitchell, I actually think this is the best birthday present I have ever had!'

He returned her smile, his blue eyes shining. 'I'm pleased to hear that.'

She swivelled towards Abe Carter, unavoidably having to lean back in Jude's arms and rest even more fully against his chest. Once again, the sensation of being content to reside here forever overwhelmed her. She kept her tone as level as she could. 'Thank you so much, Abe.'

'My pleasure, Miss Lily.'

There was no hiding her joy as the powerful horse leisurely clip-clopped along the lane. It was without doubt the most wonderful experience of her life. But deep in her heart was the true reason for this rush of happiness. That reason was sitting close behind her, trapping her between his powerful thighs, holding her safely and securely in his arms: Jude Mitchell — alas, her dear friend Prudence's suitor.

Her happiness plummeted.

★   ★   ★

She smelled of wild flowers, and her hair which blew across his face was as soft and silky as a bird's feathers. Jude hadn't expected Lily to agree to riding the horse, and he admired her for giving it a try and not worrying that she might not look ladylike, or that she might make a fool of herself.

And he had seen her delight — mingled with a little fear — as she had seated herself on Thunder's back, and his heart had swelled even more in admiration.

He only hoped that nothing else swelled as he sat here, so close that he could feel the softness of her flesh against his. It had been a long time since he had been this close to such a beautiful young woman. True enough, he hadn't been totally celibate since losing Isabella. The void she had left had been too much at times, and he had sought out a woman occasionally with whom he could sleep with. But this had been out of desperation, and although it eased the frustration of a sexless life for a time, he didn't feel particularly good about himself afterwards. Sex without love was a half-hearted thing.

Now he savoured these moments, having Lily Baines in his arms.

Although not a caress by any means, it was a closeness that excited him, inflamed him even. How wonderful if he could break through her defences, get to know her. And how miraculous if she could grow to like him, just a little. As the horse walked on, Jude allowed himself to dream — and to hope.

★　★　★

The sight of the carriage standing lopsided in the lane came all too soon. The ride on Thunder and the intimate proximity of being enclosed within Jude Mitchell's arms and legs was a sensation that she would remember for a long time. Although good sense told her that really she would be wise to try and forget it. Once he saw Prudence, he would have no interest in her at all.

Knowing Prudence, she would be instantly attracted to Jude. How could she not be? And, as he was a friend of Prudence's father, he was a suitable candidate for a husband. There was nothing to stand in their way. Even if she was to warn Prudence that he was a womaniser, she doubted that Prudence would listen or pay any attention. Prudence judged a person by their appearance and their wealth. And Jude Mitchell was top-notch in both. It was a match made in heaven.

Somehow, Lily was going to have to accept that and be happy for them both. But right at that moment, she had no idea how she was going to do this.

Abe Carter held Thunder's bridle while Jude dismounted. Then Jude reached up to Lily, his hands encircling her slender waist. Putting her trust in him, she slid from Thunder's back and into his arms. For a moment, as their bodies brushed against one another, the shivers that ran through her loins almost made her gasp. He set her down on the ground but seemed in no hurry to release her from his arms.

Lily knew she ought to instantly step away from him, but she loved the feel of his chest under her palms. There was an awakening deep inside her, a fierce desire to be held and touched and kissed. It was insanity. And, like a soap-sud bubble popping, she came to her senses and stepped free of him, moving well away.

'I hope that was a pleasurable experience for you, Lily,' he said, his blue eyes sparkling, as if he'd just galloped across the heath on a swift stallion rather than taken a slow plod on a Shire horse.

'It certainly was,' agreed Lily, side-stepping Jude to stroke Thunder's nose, needing to put some distance between them. Her body was on fire from his touch. She wanted more — but it could not be. She forced herself to be strong and detached. 'Thank you, Abe, I'll never forget this.'

'My pleasure,' said the burly black-smith as he took charge of the situation. On his instructions, the carriage driver unhitched his horses, and then Thunder was harnessed in their place. The powerful animal made short work of pulling the carriage out of the deep rut. In no time, the two coach horses were back in place, and Jude Mitchell was rewarding Abe generously, brushing off the coachman's protests that it was *he* who should pay for the blacksmith's efforts.

'It is done,' Jude dismissed, thanking Abe and slapping the Shire horse's flanks as he was led back towards the village. He turned to Lily. 'Can I give you a ride back to the manor house in the carriage, Lily?'

To be tucked up inside the close confines of the cab with him was more than appealing, and Lily glanced briefly through the open carriage door, imagining them both snug inside there, with the door closed and not a soul to see them. Her thoughts and fantasies soared for a second. What might they do? Would he reach for her, take her into his arms, kiss her passionately . . .

She drew back, embarrassed at where her thoughts were leading her. What on earth was happening to her? Besides, she could just imagine the look of disapproval on Lady Hester's face if she were to arrive with their guest — with Prudence's suitor — in such an intimate style.

'Thank you, but no,' she said, her chin tilted, her shawl clutched to her throat. 'I've left an entire basket of apples in the orchard. I need to retrieve them.'

'Alas, your restful afternoon dissolved into turmoil. I am sorry.' He didn't look sorry as he took the hand that wasn't clutching her shawl and protecting her modesty, and brought it up to his lips, his eyes glinting with desire into hers.

The fluttering was back inside her abdomen, and Lily wondered if this was how her mother had felt with her father? Was there a fierce uncontrollable passion that could not be quenched? She pulled her hand free from his with a little too much fervour, annoyed with herself for falling for his flirtatious ways. She had to face facts. He was about to meet Prudence — beautiful, adorable Prudence. Everyone loved Prudence, and there was no reason why he would not love her too.

'There is no need for apologies.' Her words came out stiffly, sounding to her own ears like they were spoken by some prim schoolmistress. 'I'm glad to have been able to help.'

'Then I thank you, Lily, from the bottom of my heart. And I shall see you again soon, at the manor?'

'No doubt,' she murmured, avoiding his gaze. It was too much. *He* was too much. And the tangled emotions running riot inside her breast were too much.

'I shall look forward to that.'

Lily turned abruptly away. I wonder if you will, she thought as she walked back up the hill. I wonder if you will even give me a second thought once you've seen Prudence?

4

'We were about to send out a search party!' Mrs Pritchard said as Lily walked into the warm kitchen, her basket filled to the brim with large green apples.

The kitchen always smelled homely with the aromas of cooking, whether it was pies or cakes. Today it was roast chicken, but oddly for Lily, she seemed to have lost her appetite. After washing her hands, she began making the pastry for the apple pie, guessing that Jude Mitchell would right this very minute be getting acquainted with Prudence.

Lily was just peeling apples when Dorothy, the maid, came bursting into the kitchen, her feet skidding on the red-tiled floor.

'You'll never guess!'

Lily most certainly *could* guess. Those flushed cheeks had been caused by the attentions of one man. And Lily felt ridiculously gullible to know she had also been blushing like a fifteen-year-old after a smile from Jude Mitchell.

The maid clasped her hands. 'Oh, Lily, Mrs Pritchard, you should see Miss Prudence's suitor. He is a dreamboat. I swear I have never seen such a handsome man.'

Lily silently groaned. She would have told Mrs Pritchard about the afternoon's events, only not now. Not when Dorothy was also so enraptured by him.

Mrs Pritchard raised her eyebrows disapprovingly and carried on whisking butter and eggs in a bowl. 'Well, I hope his presence isn't going to make you silly, Dorothy. I don't want you dropping trays at dinnertime. Maybe Lily will give you a hand to take dinner in later.' She smiled a rosy smile at Lily. 'An ounce of prevention is worth a pound of cure, and you've got a far more sensible head on your shoulders, I'm glad to say. Dorothy Brown, you'd do well to try and conduct yourself like Lily. You don't see her getting into a flap just because we have a handsome man calling.'

Dorothy was still almost swooning. 'You wait till you've seen him. Honestly, Mrs Pritchard, he'd even make your old heart flutter.'

'Less of your cheek, young lady!' scolded the cook good-naturedly. 'Now, there are potatoes and carrots waiting to be peeled. Idle hands . . .'

'Yes, I know. They're the devil's playthings.'

Lily really didn't want to be discussing the virtues of Jude Mitchell. What she wanted was to rid him from her head completely. But there was no respite as Dorothy chatted on about Jude Mitchell's hair and his deep blue eyes and the way he smiled. Once the apple pie was in the oven, Lily escaped to her bedroom on the top floor of the manor house, glad to reach the sanctuary of her room without encountering anyone else, and in particular Jude Mitchell.

Butterflies were dancing in her stomach knowing he was here in the house — probably in the drawing room, working his charms on Prudence and Lady Hester. And knowing Prudence, she would be flirting outrageously back. It just didn't bear thinking about.

Lily closed her bedroom door on the world and picked up the book that had been her birthday gift from the family that morning. She sat on her narrow bed with its knitted patchwork quilt that she had made herself, and thought back to that morning, before her life had been turned upside down.

Summoned to the drawing room, Sir Joseph had presented her with a package wrapped in brown paper and tied with a thin red ribbon. His voice had been kindly, as always, so different from his wife's sharp tongue.

'A very happy birthday, Lily,' he had said, covering her hand briefly with his as he'd given her the gift. 'I can't believe you're eighteen already. And just look at you. You've grown into a very beautiful young woman.'

'Thank you all, so much,' Lily had answered, not allowing the sour expression on Hester's face to spoil her happiness. She guessed by the weight and shape of the gift that it was a book.

'Hurry up and open it, Lily!' Prudence had exclaimed. 'I need you to help me choose what to wear to meet my suitor.'

Sir Joseph had patted his daughter's hand. 'Patience, my dear. Let Lily enjoy the moment. You've all day to prepare yourself.'

Prudence had hopped from one dainty foot to the other. 'But I'm so excited. Papa, tell me again what my suitor is like. I hope he doesn't have spots like the last one.'

Sir Joseph had smiled indulgently. 'I'm sure he doesn't. And, well, Jude is a good man, or I would not allow him within a hundred miles of you. Now, have a little patience.'

'How handsome is he?' Prudence

wanted to know. 'And how rich?'

Hester, a statuesque woman almost as tall as her husband, had stood rigid and unsmiling, clearly finding it a chore to be doling out presents to someone who was neither family nor staff. Her voice was clipped as she said, 'Jude Mitchell has taken over his late father's fleet of cargo ships and owns a large house in Whitechapel — I think he will make the perfect son-in-law.'

Seeing the focus was once again on Prudence, Lily had clutched the new book to her breast and thanked them all for their generosity.

Hester had nodded her acknowledgements as if they were only to be expected. And then, the ordeal over, their duty fulfilled for another year, she flashed a 'follow me' look at her husband and effectively steered him from the room, her grey taffeta dress rustling as stiffly as her demeanour.

The moment her parents were gone, Prudence had declared, 'Oh Lily, how dreadfully dreary — a book!'

Her disdain came as no surprise. A book certainly wasn't the sort of birthday present Prudence would receive. Her parents indulged her with lavish jewellery and clothing, but for Lily this was perfect.

With a sigh, and the memory of Hester's words of how Jude Mitchell would make the perfect son-in-law echoing in her head, Lily got comfortable on her bed and opened the book.

Inside the front cover was an inscription in Sir Joseph's hand and dated 20th September 1830. It read: 'To Lily on the occasion of her 18th birthday, with much affection, Joseph, Hester and Prudence Westfall.'

Sir Joseph had always encouraged her to read, draw and paint. While demonstrations of affection were few and far between, he took a keen interest in her education and recognised her skills as an artist. Sometimes he would slip her a new sketchpad or paints or pencils. They were always given secretly, when Hester and Prudence weren't about.

'Between you and me, Lily,' he would whisper, tapping the side of his nose conspiratorially. Lily guessed he had been the one to choose her gift today rather than Hester.

She smoothed her hand over the beige cover with its embossed title, *Thomas Beswick's A History of British Birds*. It was a wonderful gift — definitely Sir Joseph's choice.

A moment later, her bedroom door opened and Prudence popped her head around.

'There you are, Lily!' She came in, closing the door behind her, her blue eyes sparkling. 'Oh! Lily, I am in love!'

How quickly Jude had worked his magic, Lily thought, unable to even humour her friend by pretending to be pleased for her. She turned the page of her book and stared at the picture of a peacock. 'Prudence, you've known him all of what? An hour?'

'An hour, a minute, the blinking of an eye. Oh Lily, I can't wait for you to meet him. Lily, are you listening to me?'

Without warning, she snatched the book from Lily's hands. 'Will you please stop reading that dreary book while I'm talking to you?'

Prudence's actions came as no surprise, and Lily tried not to let it upset her. 'It's not in the least dreary. It's a lovely book . . . '

'Oh! Books, books and more books. Don't you ever wish you'd get a bottle of scent or a pretty bracelet?'

'Not really. I'll learn so much from studying the illustrations . . . '

Prudence tossed the book to the bottom of the bed and flopped down beside Lily. 'Enough of that, you can read it later. Right now I want to tell you about Jude. Oh, Lily, I swear it is love at first sight.'

Lily looked steadily into her friend's excited face. 'You can't possibly know enough about him to have fallen in love.'

'I know how he makes me feel, Lily. Inside . . . down here.' And she squeezed her hands down between her legs. 'I swear, if Mama and Papa had not been there, he would have taken me in his arms. Oh! The way he looked at me with those deep blue eyes . . . '

Lily's tone was so brittle when she spoke it was a wonder her words didn't splinter into shards of glass. 'Men like that are shallow womanisers. You should be careful, Prudence. You don't want your heart broken.'

Prudence's full lips turned into a pout. 'I know you mean well, Lily, but don't be such a grouch. Be happy for me. My suitor is entirely suitable!' She laughed at her own joke. 'Now come and help me dress for dinner.'

The prospect of helping Prudence to look even more beautiful for Jude sent Lily's heart spiralling downwards. Her lack of enthusiasm caused Prudence to cast her a curious look, and then she was holding Lily by both hands and pulling her to her feet.

'I thought I'd wear the blue gown at dinner.'

Lily was practically dragged out of

her bedroom, but on the landing, Prudence stopped and lowered her voice, her head close to Lily's. 'Mama has put him in *that* bedroom,' she whispered, nodding her ringletted head towards the door directly opposite Lily's. 'So don't be surprised if I'm paying you more visits than usual!'

The prospect of Jude being just across the landing sent shivers through Lily's body, and she knew precisely what Prudence had meant when she'd said how he made her feel — *down there*.

'Is he in his room now?' Lily couldn't stop herself from asking.

'No. He and Papa are in the library. Talking man-to-man.' She giggled. 'About me, I hope!'

Lily had no doubt that Prudence's assumption was correct, and it saddened her to know that she'd been right — once he'd set eyes on Prudence, Jude Mitchell wouldn't have given *her* a second thought.

Prudence grabbed Lily's hand again.

'Come on, I need you to make me look breathtaking. I want this man, Lily. I want him more than I've ever wanted anything in my whole life.'

As Lily was practically dragged back to Prudence's bedroom, she was reminded that for as long as she could remember, whatever Prudence wanted, Prudence got. This would be no different. Somehow she had to get Jude Mitchell out of her mind or she was going to end up heartbroken.

Prudence's bedroom was as bright and as frilly as Prudence herself. Eagerly, she flung open the double doors of her ornately carved oak wardrobe to reveal a row of silk, taffeta and satin gowns. Then, leaving Lily to select her clothing, she checked her reflection in the long oval mirror. 'The royal blue gown, yes?'

'No, I don't think so,' Lily replied, looking for something less revealing than the infamous royal blue gown.

'Why ever not?'

'Because the last time you wore it,

your gentleman caller's eyes nearly popped out of his head.'

Prudence laughed mischievously. 'All the more reason! I want to make an impression on Jude. I want him to *desire* me!'

The words cut through Lily like a knife. She concentrated on the rack of silky gowns, afraid that if she were to look at Prudence now, her friend would see the misery in her face — and know.

'The scarlet gown, then?' suggested Prudence. 'It has such a deliciously naughty scoop to the neckline.'

Lily brought out a lace blouse with a high collar and matching skirt in an embroidered ivory silk. 'This is lovely, and not so revealing.'

'Oh, Lily! Why must you always be so dull and sensible? I want to look ravishing for my future husband.'

Lily bit her lip, knowing this was a futile battle. Jude Mitchell was here to woo Prudence, and she had to get used to the idea. But still, Prudence was her dear friend, and was on the brink of making a dreadful mistake if she thought Jude would make a trustworthy husband.

Prudence held a green-and-black taffeta dress up against her, viewing herself from all angles in the full-length mirror. 'I wonder what Jude's favourite colour is? Oh, Lily, can you imagine — Mrs Prudence Mitchell!'

'Prudence, please don't rush into anything. You don't know him well enough. He might break your heart.'

Irritated suddenly, Prudence thrust the garment into Lily's arms. 'What has got into you? Anyone would think you didn't want me to be happy.'

Lily suddenly realised how selfish she was being. This afternoon's events should never have happened. Jude was here for Prudence, and whether he was a womaniser or not, that was up to Prudence to discover for herself. She took a deep breath, then squeezed her friend's hands. 'Of course I want you to be happy. I'm just being overly protective, I suppose.'

Prudence hugged her, her eyes shining with happiness, and Lily wondered whether Jude had already fallen under her spell. She was pretty, she was feminine, and she was fun. How could he not fall for her?

Clasping her dainty hands to her mouth, Prudence drifted off into another dreamy trance. 'He has the bluest of eyes, Lily, you should see them. I swear they are like sapphires. His hair is a little long, but I'm sure he will soon get that cut when I tell him to.'

Lily caught her breath, wondering what right Prudence had to dictate what style of hair a man like Jude Mitchell should have. But of course Prudence would soon have every right. If Jude liked her — and how could he not? — then he and she would be man and wife, and she could dictate whatever she wanted.

There was a tight feeling in Lily's throat, and she had difficulty in smiling, in pretending to be delighted. She did her best not to give away her feelings. 'And your parents — does Sir Joseph and Hester approve of him?'

'Oh yes, most certainly. I could tell by the way Mama was fawning over him — you know, how she does when any decent-looking gentleman is around. Honestly, the way she was fussing over him, it was a wonder Papa wasn't jealous.'

'That's excellent, then,' murmured Lily, truly wishing that she meant it.

After assisting Prudence in trying on practically every lush gown in her wardrobe, she had eventually settled on the seductive royal blue gown with the low-cut neckline and laced-up corseted bodice. She could just imagine how enraptured Jude Mitchell would be when he saw Prudence in this.

Feeling quite out of sorts, Lily went back down to the kitchen. There was plenty to do, seeing as their guest was staying indefinitely.

Lily had spent many an hour in the kitchen with Mrs Pritchard, learning how to cook and keep a good kitchen store cupboard. Perhaps, one day, she would be a housekeeper or a cook. Although her secret passion was to use her artistic skills — to be an illustrator, maybe. How wonderful that would be! But she had no idea how to go about such a career. Besides, she doubted she was skilled enough anyway.

Usually, as she helped Mrs Pritchard, they would talk, often about her mother. The cook had been here when Lillian Baines had been the scullery maid. It was through Mrs Pritchard that Lily had learned something of her mother. Sir Joseph and Hester had told her very little over the years. For them, it was as if the subject should be brushed under the carpet. Gradually, however, Lily was building up a picture of the mother she had never known.

According to Mrs Pritchard, Lily looked more like her mother every day. The same golden-coloured hair which, if left to its own devices, bounced around her shoulders in long twists like barley-sugar canes. Her slender figure and posture were much like her mother's too.

'You even walk like your mother,' Mrs Pritchard had told her one day, and when Lily had asked what she meant, she'd said, 'Well, you have a sway to the hips that some men might find a bit . . . well, you know, saucy.'

It had horrified her. 'Do I? I don't mean to.'

'And you have a way of looking at people from under your eyelashes. Your mother did that too. Flirty, some would call it.'

That had horrified her even more and she had protested, 'But I'm not a flirt.'

'I'm not saying you are, my dear. I'm saying how it appears.'

'Was my mother a flirt?' Lily had asked.

Mrs Pritchard had given her a hug. 'Your mother was a hardworking young woman. She only got one afternoon off a week, and she was so tired she'd spend that in her room. I've pondered many a time how she managed to get herself into trouble with you in the first place.'

On past occasions, the cook had also told her that she'd got her mother's smile and laugh; although Lily wasn't sure if that was a desirable thing or not, as on one occasion when she had been laughing at the antics of the family's cat, pouncing on a ray of sunlight playing through the French windows, Hester had snapped, 'Enough of your cackling!' and jabbed Lily so hard and so suddenly in the ribs it had brought tears to her eyes.

'You're very quiet today, Lily.' Mrs Pritchard's voice broke through her thoughts.

She jumped slightly as she mixed egg yolks, sugar and milk for the custard later. 'Am I? Sorry . . . '

The cook gave Lily a hug. 'I know what you're thinking, my dear.'

Lily hoped it wasn't obvious that she couldn't get Prudence's suitor out of her mind. She was relieved when Mrs Pritchard said, 'It's natural to think of your mother, this being her anniversary.'

Lily nodded, and said nothing to the contrary.

'Anyway, we've a special treat later once we've cleared away after *their* meal.'

'Really? What is it?'

Dorothy who had been stirring the gravy, turned to beam at her. 'We've made a special birthday cake for you, with almonds and crystal ginger and cherries . . . '

Mrs Pritchard lowered her voice. 'Well, seeing as *them* lot haven't made any special arrangements for your eighteenth . . . They are a bunch of cold fish at times.' She cast a warning glance at Dorothy. 'And don't you go repeating my words, madam.'

'I wouldn't dream of it, Mrs Pritchard.'

A brass bell on the kitchen wall jangled, summoning one of them to

Prudence's room.

'She'll be after you, Lily,' said the cook.

'No rest for the wicked!' Dorothy chimed out.

Apparently not, thought Lily, as she went up to Prudence's room. And obviously it was wicked to be constantly thinking about another woman's suitor.

With it being so close to dinner time, Lily half expected to bump into Jude heading into the dining room, or meet him on the stairs. But she reached Prudence's bedroom without encountering anyone.

Prudence was at her dressing table, inspecting her flawless face in the mirror. 'Ah! Lily, I need you to titivate my hair.' She angled an ornate hand mirror so she could see the back of her head. 'Are my curls still pinned nicely? You can't see the pins, can you?'

'Your hair is perfect, Prudence. There's not a single strand out of place.'

Prudence swung around on her

velvet-cushioned stool and clasped Lily's hands. 'I'm so excited at dining with him. I can't wait for you to meet him.'

Lily opened her mouth to explain that they had already met, and then snapped it shut, afraid that if she started talking about Jude, Prudence might detect her attraction to him, and that would be too awful.

'I have an idea!' exclaimed Prudence. 'Why don't you help Dorothy to serve dinner? Oh, I know it's not your job, but actually you like doing all that cooking fiddle-faddle, don't you?'

The prospect of seeing Jude again sent her emotions into turmoil. Yes, she wanted to see him, but not with him fawning over Prudence. She couldn't bear it. 'You don't want me there . . . '

'I do!' Prudence cried, jumping to her feet, her blue eyes pleading. 'It will be such fun. We can exchange glances, and you can be the judge as to how much he likes me. Now, you won't be too envious, will you?'

'I'm sure I won't!' Lily said, knowing she sounded too sharp. Smoothing her tone with a smile, she added, 'How could I be envious of you? I'll be happy for you. Very happy.'

'Oh yes, and I am happy. I think finally I have met my Prince Charming. I don't think I have ever felt happier.'

As Lily, went back downstairs to prepare for the ordeal, she realised that she couldn't think of a time when she'd felt more wretched.

5

Washed and refreshed, with a clean shirt, charcoal-grey breeches, and leather shoes rather than heavy boots for the Westfalls' elegantly polished floors and exquisite rugs, Jude prepared to go down for dinner.

It had been a good day. He couldn't remember when he'd enjoyed a day so much. It was pleasing to meet up with Sir Joseph again. He had long been a good friend of his father when he'd been alive. They had stayed in touch via letters. It had been in one of their communications that the suggestion had been made about him visiting Westfall Manor to meet Prudence.

Her mother, Lady Hester, had been utterly charming and welcoming to him. And Prudence — well, she was like a painted doll. But of course the thing that had really made his day was meeting Lily Baines. He couldn't wait to see her again.

With a glance at his reflection and hoping that he looked presentable, he went downstairs. Sir Joseph emerged from his study to greet him and lead the way into the dining room.

'A small glass of sherry?' suggested Sir Joseph, removing the stopper from a crystal decanter.

'Thank you,' said Jude. 'And I'm looking forward to seeing the estate tomorrow, as you suggested. From what you were telling me you have some excellent produce being farmed.'

'Indeed we do,' agreed Sir Joseph. 'Possibly we'll be able to work together on exporting some of our produce. But first, how about you and life on the open seas . . . ?'

'Isn't it awfully cold and wet?' asked Prudence, entering the room with her mother and catching the last part of the conversation.

Jude turned to greet them. He bowed his head slightly, finding an abundance of bosom confronting him. Prudence had certainly dressed to kill. Slightly taken aback, he managed not to stare and kept his gaze at eye-level. 'Er . . . yes, it is extremely wet and cold, but you get acclimatised to bad weather, and when the sun shines there is nowhere better to be than sailing across the ocean.'

'Are women allowed on your ships?' Lady Hester asked, as Sir Joseph poured out two more sherries.

Hester was a striking-looking woman. Jude had thought that the moment he'd set eyes on Sir Joseph's wife. But close to, he could see the harsh lines around her mouth, and he sensed that her smile was put on for his benefit.

'They are indeed, madam. But as passengers, not crew.'

'Call me Hester, please.'

'Hester,' he acknowledged. 'Yes, we have passenger — or steerage — areas below deck. So many people these days wish to travel or live abroad. Ever more so these days, as some of our ships are being fitted with steam engines — such wonderful inventions.'

'Indeed,' agreed Sir Joseph. 'We'll be seeing steam-powered vehicles on our roads before we know it.'

'Joseph,' Lady Hester cut in, 'I'm sure Mr Mitchell would much prefer talking to Prudence rather than discussing engines and the workplace. Why don't the pair of you relax on the chaise longue by the fire until dinner is served?'

It wasn't what he preferred to do, but Prudence slid her arm through his and led him towards an elaborately upholstered leather settee. She seated herself a little too close and turned slightly so that her knee, draped in blue silk, brushed against his thigh. The fact that her touch made him want to inch a little further away did not bode well for a prospective love match.

'Mr Mitchell, do tell me all about London,' said Prudence, fluttering her pretty eyelashes at him.

She was so obvious that it made him

smile. 'Well, London is a real mixture of beauty and squalor. The conditions that many poor souls live in are appalling . . . '

'I don't want to hear about *that* side of London,' Prudence interrupted. 'Tell me about the beautiful parts — Buckingham Palace and the Houses of Parliament — oh, and the Tower of London where they chop people's heads off!'

Jude took a deep breath, calming the irritation that sprung up from within. He wouldn't tell her that his wife Isabella had died of pneumonia whilst trying to help the poor of London. He wouldn't let any of them see that her comment had hit a raw nerve. Although, to give Sir Joseph his due, the man did look slightly ashamed that his daughter had come out with such a remark. Jude locked away his feelings and wondered instead whether Lily Baines had found time to bake that apple pie.

Fixing an interested, charmed expression on his face, he listened to

Prudence and her mother prattle on about London fashions — and thought about Lily.

* * *

It seemed there was to be no escaping the ordeal of serving dinner. It was what Prudence wanted, and Mrs Pritchard also wanted Lily to assist Dorothy in serving the evening meal. 'She needs a good level-headed young woman like you as a guiding light, Lily,' she'd said.

The prospect of coming face to face with Jude Mitchell again made Lily feel anything but level-headed. It made her heart race and butterflies flutter in her stomach.

In readiness to help serve dinner, Lily had changed into a long navy skirt and white blouse — with all of its buttons fastened. She'd also found time to sew new buttons onto the blouse she'd worn earlier before depositing it into the laundry basket. She had brushed the tangles from her long hair and clipped it neatly into a twist at the back of her head. Now, as she placed two large rose-patterned china dishes filled with carrots and potatoes onto a tray, she did her best to adopt an emotionless expression, and prayed the colour would not rush up into her cheeks on seeing Jude Mitchell again.

Mrs Pritchard held the kitchen door open for Dorothy to lead the way. Her tray was laden with a steaming roast chicken and the gravy boat, the aroma from which was heavenly. 'Off you go now, Dorothy. Keep your mind on what you're doing. And thank you, Lily. One volunteer is worth twenty pressed men!'

Dorothy led the way along the hallway, placed her tray on the slender walnut table near the dining room entrance to open the door, then proceeded into the room. Lily followed, keeping her eyes fixed on the back of Dorothy's head, not allowing her gaze to roam around the elegant room.

In all her eighteen years she had never eaten in this room with the family. She had always taken her meals in the kitchen with Mrs Pritchard and whichever maid had been working here. The cook had a way of training up the scullery maids, so upon reaching eighteen or nineteen they were all set to go out and find employment as a housekeeper or cook at another establishment. No doubt her own mother would have had that opportunity — if things had not ended so tragically.

From the corner of her eye, Lily sensed the four were seated to her right, around the stone fireplace. Summoning up every ounce of willpower, she stopped herself from glancing over, but she knew precisely that Jude and Prudence were sitting close together on the chaise longue, and Sir Joseph was relaxing in his favourite high-backed leather armchair, with Lady Hester upright on the edge of her seat. The happy family all together — welcoming their prospective new son-in-law into the fold. Lily tried hard not to let it bother her.

'Ah! Dinner is served!' announced Sir Joseph, getting to his feet. 'Fresh roast chicken from Ted Draper's farm — I'll introduce you to him tomorrow, Jude.'

Observing Dorothy's actions of setting the trays down and arranging the food in the centre of the table, Lily was eager to get away. Even being in the same room as Jude Mitchell was unsettling. Turning to make her escape, Prudence caught her eye and shot a wide-eyed glance towards the man sitting next to her. Lily pretended not to have noticed, and more especially avoided Jude's eye as he looked her way.

The young maid bobbed a curtsey and left. Lily went to do likewise, acutely aware now that Jude's gaze was burning through her — unless it was just her imagination. Probably, if she risked glancing at the family, who all seemed to be focused on her now, she would see they were actually all just looking at the food laid out for them. Probably Jude Mitchell had forgotten all about their little interlude earlier. She was almost out of the door when Prudence called her back.

'Lily, do come and meet Mr Mitchell.'

She caught her breath. There was no escape. She was going to have to face him and speak to him. The prospect of putting on some pretence of disinterest with everyone watching was utterly daunting. She was terrified they'd see there had already been a connection. That they'd been so physically close; that she knew the feel of those arms around her, and those powerful thighs gripping her. She knew how it felt to rest back against his muscular body, and the sensation of his kiss on the back of her hand. Heat rose inside her as she took a deep breath and forced a pleasant but disinterested expression onto her face.

To her alarm, Jude was already

crossing the room. In two strides he was beside her, and her hand was clasped between his. 'But we have already met!'

Lily distinctly heard the sharp intake of breath from both Hester and Prudence, and practically felt as if a cold wind had swept through the room.

'You have?' Hester murmured, rising to her feet, her face like stone.

'Lily?' Prudence uttered, the word coming out like the whine of a kitten with an injured paw. 'You didn't tell me.'

Jude was still holding her hand like they were long-lost friends, and his touch was causing tiny bolts of lightning to dart through her, making every nerve ending in her body tingle. She dragged her hand free, sensing Hester and Prudence's accusing eyes on her. She tried to shrug and smile innocently. 'There is nothing to tell.' But she felt far from innocent.

'Nothing?' Jude exclaimed in astonishment, placing an arm around the small of her back and drawing her into the centre of the room. 'I have to tell you that this astonishing, brave young woman defied death and injury this afternoon . . . '

'I did nothing of the sort,' Lily protested, her cheeks on fire.

'You are too modest, Lily,' said Jude, glancing from her to the family and then settling those dazzling blue eyes back on her. 'This young woman risked life and limb to save me and the carriage driver from the raging hooves of his horses.'

He was being ridiculously overly dramatic, just as he had been when he told the story to Abe Carter. But if he had hoped for the same reaction, he was in for a disappointment. Hester and Prudence both had sour looks on their faces. Only Sir Joseph seemed intrigued.

'Travelling along at quite a speed, our carriage stuck a pothole in the road and came to a sudden and bone-jarring halt,' Jude explained, not releasing his hold on her for a second, and his admiring glances continually suggesting that he was truly in awe of her actions. The expressions of Prudence and her mother were turning more frosty by the second.

'The poor driver was thrown practically under the horses' hooves. They were panicking and rearing, and there was nothing I could do to calm them, when out of the blue came this tower of strength and courageousness ... ' Again, another adoring look came her way, making her cringe, making her want to beg him to stop. But he was well into the story, oblivious to the effect it was having on everyone. Even Sir Joseph was looking anxiously now at his wife and daughter, observant of their change in mood.

'All I did was give him my shawl to drape over the horses' eyes,' Lily protested, the combination of embarrassment and nerves making her want to giggle.

Hester pursed her lips, hands locked

in front of her stiff torso. 'Pray do continue, Mr Mitchell. We are all ears.'

'Yes, all ears,' agreed Prudence, her lower lip pouting.

'I would never have thought of doing that,' continued Jude, his hand remaining at the curve of her spine, totally unaware of her embarrassment or the hostility of the two other women in the room. 'As if by magic, the horses calmed down. It's usual for a gentleman to rescue a damsel in distress, not for the damsel to rescue the men. And then, as if that wasn't enough — '

'Yes?' Prudence asked sulkily. 'What else did Lily do? Pray tell!'

Lily stepped towards her, attempting to hold Prudence's hand and assure her she had done nothing deliberately to gain her suitor's admiration. But Prudence pulled her hands away and tucked them behind her back, her glare so hostile and angry that it took Lily aback.

There was a slight pause before Jude took up the story again. 'She kindly introduced me to Abe Carter the blacksmith . . . '

Lily interrupted, terrified that he would tell of them both riding Thunder back from the village. Desperately, she took up the conversation. 'His horse soon had the carriage righted. It's such a powerful animal. Have you ever noticed him, Prudence? He's called Thunder . . . '

'I have no interest in horses. They bite and they kick.' Prudence linked her arm through her mother's, looking mortally wounded. 'So you escorted Mr Mitchell into the village to get help; how kind.'

'Indeed, she was,' agreed Jude, undeterred that his was the only cheerful face in the room. In fact it was only Sir Joseph who wasn't actually scowling, although his eyebrows were drawn together, as if his head ached suddenly.

Lily felt their anger from where she stood. If the daggers in their eyes had been real then she would be lying dead on the floor! Why, oh why, couldn't Jude see what he was doing? The man was completely oblivious to the effect this story was having upon his hosts.

'This young woman deserves a medal for bravery,' Jude continued, smiling directly at her now, with such obvious affection that under different circumstances it would have made her heart sing. But all she wanted to do was crawl away and die.

'Mama!' Prudence bleated, and Hester immediately disentangled herself from her daughter's hold and marched straight at Lily.

For a second Lily flinched, fully expecting an angry slap from the woman. Whether Jude sensed her body tensing, she had no idea. All she knew was that Hester was furious. Yet her voice, amazingly, was coated in honey.

'Such bravery, indeed. You must be congratulated. But for now, our guest is in need of sustenance. You may go, Lily.'

Hester took her arm, her grip unduly

fierce, drawing her away from Jude and propelling her towards the door. She was out into the hallway in a second, the door closing behind her with a resounding bang. Lily stood trembling from head to toe. For a moment she was quite stunned, and then she began to feel annoyed. The man was totally insensitive. Why hadn't he realised the effect his story would have on everyone? No doubt it was nothing but an amusing incident that he would tell a hundred times over to entertain his friends, and no doubt it would become more embellished with every telling. But for her it was humiliating and distressing. She owed the Westfalls so much for giving her a good home all these years. They would have been quite within their rights to have sent her to an orphanage, or even the workhouse. But they hadn't. They had given her a good home, good food and a good education. And Prudence was her dear friend. She felt as if she had betrayed them all.

Why on earth she had thought herself

attracted to Jude Mitchell, she didn't know. He was an insensitive, self-centred womaniser. She hated the man.

6

The fury Jude felt burned like a flame deep in his chest. How he kept from showing it, he didn't know. Fair enough, Lily Baines was just one of their servants, but for them to become so annoyed with her for — what? For becoming acquainted with him without their say-so? Did they already think he was their possession? Well, they were sadly mistaken.

He really didn't know how he managed to refrain from showing the sudden anger that had rushed up from nowhere as Lily had been ejected from the room. Somehow he had remained passive, attentive to his hosts, coaxing a smile back onto Prudence's pouting, sulky face. Sir Joseph had tried to act as if nothing was wrong. He'd cheerfully ushered everyone to the table and carved the chicken, talking as if they were all in good spirits.

Jude had done his best to pretend to have ignored the situation, but he didn't care to see anyone treated unfairly, and he particularly didn't like to see Lily treated in such a manner.

He was glad to have food set before him, as it gave him the chance to remain silent for a while as everyone ate. Slowly, his fury abated, and he realised it had been a long time since he had felt such a variety of emotions — hope, earlier; and happiness; and now anger. For the last two years, since Isabella died, he hadn't felt passionate about anything. For much of the time until today he'd felt as if his body and spirit were numb, emotionless, and would remain so until his dying day. He had thought that there was nothing in life to get worked up about. But suddenly that had all changed. It shocked him to feel so emotional. And while the anger hadn't been a good feeling, it was a passion of sorts. He felt alive again. Perhaps life was worth living after all. And he had one woman to thank for that. Lily Baines.

'More potatoes, Mr Mitchell?'

'Thank you, I will,' said Jude, enjoying the meal, if not the company so much now. 'And the chicken is delicious.' He glanced across the table to Prudence. 'You haven't eaten very much.'

She dabbed her lips with a napkin. 'My appetite has left me, I fear.'

'And why is that?' he asked, raising one eyebrow as he waited for some petulant response.

Lady Hester stepped in. 'Pray, tell us all about your shipping company, Mr Mitchell. My husband informs me you have a fleet of cargo ships that sail the globe. Do you sail with them, or are you shut away in some stuffy office all day long?'

'I make time to go out with my ships, as my dear father did, until his tragic death,' he answered, his thoughts drifting back to the storm when his father had drowned while trying to save a crew member who had been washed overboard. And then, so soon afterwards, poor Isabella had passed away too.

'A tragedy indeed,' agreed Sir Joseph. 'Your father was a fine man.'

'Indeed,' agreed Jude, trying not to dwell on the ache in his heart that was never far away. He took a steadying breath. 'So, just as my father did, I like to keep a close eye on the conditions the men sail under. And, of course, these are exciting times. You tend to think you know what you're importing from distant shores, but I like to see for myself, and to satisfy myself that nothing I import has come through slave labour. It's not been so long since slavery was abolished in this country. But sadly it still goes on elsewhere.'

Across the table, Prudence sat in the most ridiculous of postures, with her back so straight that her breasts looked like platforms on which you might balance your teacup. And while he certainly recognised an attractive woman, he preferred seduction to be a little more subtle. His mind drifted to Lily again, realising that she had seduced him without even knowing it.

'What I don't understand,' said Prudence, nibbling on a tiny piece of chicken. 'is what difference does it make if something has been grown or made by slaves or by anyone else? It's the product that counts, after all.'

Jude could scarcely believe his ears. But he was thankful that it wasn't left to him to say anything as Sir Joseph, coughing with embarrassment, spoke up swiftly.

'My daughter has led a somewhat sheltered life. I'm afraid that I'm to blame in keeping some of the less pleasant side of life away from her.'

'What?' Prudence asked innocently. 'I'm sure I should like to have my own slave.'

Hester laughed loudly. 'She is such a wit. Do tell us more about your work, Jude.'

He wondered if Hester knew how

pinched her face looked when she put on that false smile. He had thought her quite beautiful upon first meeting. Now he saw that her beauty was just skin-deep. And clearly her silly daughter was just the same.

He acknowledged Sir Joseph's excuses for his daughter's comments, almost pitying the man for having such a pretty daughter who had little to offer apart from her very obvious charms. For the remainder of the meal he talked of the different countries he had visited, places he had seen and customs he had learnt about, regaling them with humorous stories.

Eventually, Sir Joseph said wistfully, 'I envy you, Jude. I rarely travel beyond the county boundaries, let alone to another country.'

'Then you are missing out, sir,' said Jude, feeling truly sorry for the man.

Prudence reached over to her father and squeezed his hand. It seemed more like a ploy for his attention rather than a gesture of empathy. 'Papa likes to be here with his family, don't you, Papa?'

'Of course,' he answered patting her hand affectionately.

'Anyway,' Prudence continued, looking directly at him, 'Mama and I know that the high seas are dangerous. I should hate it. I've heard that you can get terribly seasick.'

'You can indeed, Prudence,' Jude said, smiling indulgently at her. She was a very pretty young woman, but as shallow as a puddle on a summer's day. He had made a mistake agreeing to meet Sir Joseph's daughter — a massive mistake. There was certainly a woman here who did interest him, but it definitely wasn't Prudence.

He longed to see Lily again. Like an actual itch that desperately needed scratching, he could happily have marched straight out of here and ripped the house apart until he found her. But good manners and respect for his father's old friend stopped him from doing so.

With the main meal finished, Hester

rang a bell, which he guessed would summon someone up from the kitchen to clear away the dishes and then bring their pudding. He fervently hoped it would be Lily; and if it was, he certainly wasn't going to ignore her, whether it irritated Lady Hester and Prudence or not.

However, it wasn't Lily. It was the younger maid. Somehow he hid his disappointment, but enjoyed the apple pie and custard immensely, especially knowing that it was Lily's fair hands that had made it.

* * *

'Whatever is the matter, Lily?' Mrs Pritchard puzzled after all the dishes had been washed up from the family's meal and there was time now to sit down to their own dinner around the scrubbed oak table.

She had forced herself to eat, her appetite quite deserting her.

'I don't like to see you looking so out

of sorts,' the cook continued. 'Are you thinking of your mother, or has someone upset you?'

Lily wished now she'd told Mrs Pritchard about meeting Jude earlier. At least then she could tell her about the family's anger and get some sort of guidance.

Dorothy jumped up from the table. 'I know how to bring a smile back to Lily's face. May I fetch the birthday cake, Mrs Pritchard?'

'Indeed you can, Dorothy. And plates and forks.'

Lily had quite forgotten that they'd made her a cake, and when Dorothy carried it out from the larder, Lily gasped in delight. 'Oh! It's wonderful!'

'There! That's better,' Mrs Pritchard said happily. 'I don't care to see you looking so glum.'

Lily's spirits lifted as she cut everyone a large slice of cake, and they tucked in with a nice cup of tea.

Someone tapped the kitchen door as they were on to their second slice. They all looked around to find Sir Joseph standing there.

'May I join the party?'

The cook and Dorothy got to their feet, and even Lily was surprised that he should venture into the kitchen. It was a room he rarely visited. Lily assumed it was something to do with her speaking to Jude earlier. She only hoped she wasn't in more trouble.

'Please, sit down,' said Sir Joseph. 'My, that cake looks tempting.'

Mrs Pritchard went to cut him a slice, but he patted his waistline. 'Better not. I just had two helpings of apple pie.'

'Our Lily made that,' said Mrs Pritchard proudly.

'It was delicious, Lily. We all enjoyed it very much.'

'Thank you,' she murmured, unable to imagine why he was here. He didn't seem annoyed with her. In fact, he was never annoyed or sharp with her. He had always been kind — distant, but kind.

He glanced over his shoulder as if expecting Hester to come looking for him, then took something from his waistcoat pocket. He lowered his voice and tapped his nose. 'I have something for you, Lily. Don't let on to *them*.'

She knew that *them* meant his wife and daughter. She frowned. He couldn't bring a sketchpad and pencils from a small waistcoat pocket. And then she saw it was a small gold cross on a slender chain. He placed it in her hand. It was light and delicately engraved in a vine leaf pattern.

'It was your mother's.'

Lily gasped. 'My mother's!'

Behind her, she heard Mrs Pritchard draw in her breath.

'As you may know, Lily,' Sir Joseph continued. 'I was with your mother in her last hours. She didn't die alone, don't ever think that. I was with her. I held her in my arms as she slipped away. But before she passed over, she asked me to give you her cross and chain when you were eighteen.'

119

Tears welled up in Lily's eyes so that the sparkling gold shimmered and blurred. 'Thank you.'

'My wife has never known about this cross, Lily. And I don't want her to know that I've been keeping it safe for you all these years. As you've probably gathered, she and Prudence can be a little self-centred at times.'

Lily could barely speak, and the tears she was trying to hold back suddenly streamed down her cheeks. 'It's beautiful!'

'It meant a lot to your mother, Lily. It was given to her by the man she loved — the man who loved her.' He was speaking so softly, she could only just catch his words. But then he looked her straight in the eye and said, 'Your father gave it to her.'

Lily felt the strength leave her. No one talked about her father, no one! She was almost too afraid to ask the question, but she had to. 'Did you know him? Do you know who he was . . . is?'

He hesitated for just a fleeting

second, but long enough to make Lily think that he knew the answer to her question. But then he shook his head. 'Your dear mother took that secret to the grave with her.'

She accepted this with a slight nod of her head. She wasn't disappointed — she was elated. She had the cross and chain that her mother had worn, that her father had given to her mother. It was beyond her wildest dreams.

'Here, let me put it on for you,' said Sir Joseph, taking the cross back to fasten the chain around her throat. And then he did something he had never done in all of Lily's life. He kissed her tenderly on the cheek and held her for a moment in his arms. 'Happy birthday, Lily. Your mother would be so proud of you.'

Her throat ached. Gulping back the tears, Lily managed to utter, 'Thank you.' And then he was gone.

7

Lily felt as if she were walking on air as she headed back to her bedroom. She could feel the gold cross warm against her skin: it felt like a caress, as if her mother and father were reaching out across the void to touch her. To tell her that she was loved, and it was their love for each other that had brought her into this world.

She no longer felt that she was a mistake, an accident that should never have happened — a thought which had troubled her for years.

The earlier embarrassing scene in the dining room paled almost into insignificance. And her foolish rush of attraction to Jude Mitchell was pushed to the back of her mind, where it belonged.

But then suddenly he was there in front of her. As she reached the top landing he was emerging from his bedroom, and her heart lurched inside her breast.

'Lily!' He stopped in his tracks and his blue gaze washed over her, sending unwanted tremors through her body.

'Mr Mitchell,' she said stiffly.

'Please, call me Jude,' he said, smiling into her eyes, quickening her pulse.

'That would hardly be appropriate, Mr Mitchell,' she answered, needing to get swiftly past him and into the sanctuary of her room. The man had a most undesirable effect on her. She didn't want to feel as wretched as she'd felt earlier.

But he seemed in no hurry to let her pass. 'No, it probably wouldn't, particularly if the other ladies of the house were to hear you.' He gave her a rueful smile. 'I hope you will forgive me if I embarrassed you earlier. I never meant to. I was expecting them to be as impressed with you as I was.'

'Well, it's over and done with now,

Mr Mitchell. We can put it all behind us.'

'The apple pie was delicious, by the way. The best I've ever tasted.'

'Thank you. I'm glad you enjoyed it,' Lily dismissed, trying to dip past him.

His hand moved to rest lightly on her forearm, taking her totally by surprise. 'I would enjoy your company even more, Lily.'

Her breath caught in her throat. She went to speak, to remind him that he was here for Prudence, and she wouldn't stand to see her dear friend made a fool of by his philandering. But then she spotted Prudence running up the stairs, holding on to the hem of her gown, her head down, ringlets bobbing.

'Jude! There you are!' Prudence exclaimed, looking up and spotting him. Then, seeing Lily, her expression soured. 'And Lily too! My goodness, we can't keep you two apart, can we?'

Lost for words, and still stunned by Jude Mitchell's unspeakable behaviour, Lily bid Prudence goodnight and escaped swiftly into her room. She leant against the door, aware of them talking on the landing, her own heart pounding fiercely.

'We've been waiting for you in the drawing room,' said Prudence. 'I'm to sing for you.'

'I apologise for keeping you waiting,' Jude replied, and then their voices faded as they went downstairs together.

Lily sat down on the edge of her bed, trembling from the effects of the man. Goodness, what was wrong with her? Why, oh why, was he having such a devastating effect on her? She had to get her emotions under control. And he had to stop flirting with her!

Alone in her room, she stripped out of her rather formal skirt and blouse and into a loose-fitting nightgown that was scooped at the neck. She took the pins from her hair, glad to be able to shake it free and let it fall around her shoulders. Picking up a hand mirror and brush, she caught sight of the gold cross in her reflection. Putting down the brush, she ran her fingers over the cross, imagining her mother doing the same thing. This had been her room; she'd been told that. She most probably had sat in this very spot, touching this lovely cross and dreaming of her lover, just as *she* was sitting here thinking about Jude.

She halted her train of thought. This situation was nothing like her mother's circumstances. There hadn't been another woman in the picture for her mother, as far as Lily knew — unless . . .

Unless her mother had been in love with a married man, someone who wasn't free to make an honest woman out of her. Someone who wasn't free to marry her because he already had a wife. It would explain why no one knew who her father was. She'd had to keep it a secret.

The most insane thought flashed through Lily's head. She cast it aside instantly, ashamed that she should even think such a thing.

An hour or so later, as Lily was sitting in bed browsing her new book, her bedroom door burst open. She jumped, startled, as Prudence barged in.

'Prudence? Is everything all right?'

For a moment, Prudence just stood there, shuffling awkwardly from one foot to the other, a lace handkerchief gripped in her hands. Finally, she blurted out, 'Don't you think you should have told me?'

For a moment, Lily wasn't quite sure what she was referring to. So much had happened to upset the apple-cart in such a short time.

'Don't look so dumbfounded, Lily. I'm referring to you and Jude walking into the village together, returning together. You and my young man! I must say, you certainly made an impression on him. He is quite enamoured with you.'

Lily swung her legs out of bed, wanting to give Prudence a hug, needing to reassure her that she was no threat to her happiness with Jude Mitchell. In fact, she was welcome to the man.

But Prudence turned aside, her chin tilted haughtily, halting Lily in her tracks.

'I'm sure he isn't in the slightest bit interested in me,' said Lily. 'And that whole incident was something and nothing. Mr Mitchell was exaggerating for the sake of entertainment.'

Prudence stomped across the room, found herself at the far wall in only a few strides, and spun round to face Lily again. 'But you went walking with him — just the two of you. You and my suitor. The man I intend to marry.'

'Has he asked you?' The question was out before Lily could stop herself.

Prudence turned pink. 'We've had precious little time to get to know one another yet. His time has been too preoccupied with you!'

'That was totally unavoidable.'

Prudence looked like she was trying to tear her handkerchief in two. 'Yes, well, I hope it was unavoidable because I would like you to avoid him from now on.'

Lily could scarcely believe her ears. 'I'm sorry?'

'You . . . you heard me. You should avoid him. It's me he's come to see.'

Lily felt like ice water was running through her veins. 'You're telling me who I can and cannot speak to?'

Two blotches of crimson made Prudence look suddenly like a painted china doll. 'Yes! That's exactly what I'm telling you.'

'But . . . '

'But nothing! That's my orders, Lily. I suggest you do as you're told, or you can . . . you can . . . ' She didn't finish her sentence, but turned and stormed out of the room. The slamming of the door reverberated in Lily's ears long after she had gone.

It was impossible to settle. When Lily's anger at Prudence's bossiness had subsided, she started to think rationally. Of course Prudence was right. Jude was here to meet her. Prudence was Sir Joseph Westfall's daughter. This house and the estate would all be hers one day. She would make a fine wife for a wealthy businessman. Jude certainly wouldn't be interested in a little nobody like her — except perhaps to dally with.

Yet it hurt to think of Jude and Prudence married, sharing a life together. The man was inside her head. His face seemed to have etched itself onto her mind. She could see him there with every blink of her eyes. She could feel his touch. How on earth was she supposed to stop thinking about him? She would go mad trying.

With the first glimpse of dawn's silvery light, Lily rose from her bed. She had slept badly, too many conflicting thoughts running through her head. Fitful dreams of being in Jude's arms, and Prudence angrily condemning her.

During the evening she had heard Jude's footsteps on the landing. She'd thought he had hesitated before going into his room. She'd held her breath, half afraid and half longing for him to knock at her door. For one crazed moment she had even considered opening her bedroom door on the ruse of needing something from downstairs; but good sense had reigned, and so she had lain motionless in her bed, clutching the sheet to her chin and fighting back the tremors of longing that stirred deep within her. When finally she had heard him going into his room, closing his bedroom door after him, she had felt a sense of relief, but it was mingled with a twang of disappointment.

Despite her resolve to put him out of her mind, and despite Prudence's orders that she should stay well away from him, there was a part of her that was beyond good sense. That reckless spirit she guessed she had inherited from her mother.

Sleep had refused to come until the early hours, and the night had seemed endless. Now, glad of the pale morning light, she washed and dressed and brushed the tangles from her hair. She took a blanket, sketchpad and pencils, and crept from her room, glancing for a moment at the closed door of the room she knew to be Jude's.

Tiptoeing down the stairs, she avoided the creaking parts that might waken the family. She loved to be out in the early morning and was regularly the first person up. Prudence often teased her about her early-morning walks, suggesting that she was meeting up with a secret lover, and threatening to catch her out one of these days.

Wrapping a shawl around her shoulders, Lily went out of the back door into the gardens. She ran across the lawn sparkling with dew, beneath the trellised walkway smothered in fragrant pink roses, and down towards the orchard. Last evening's confrontation with Prudence was still echoing through her mind. It needled her to be told who she could and couldn't talk to. But she forced herself to remember that the Westfalls were good people. She was so lucky to live here and not to have been handed over to an orphanage or the workhouse as a baby. She would always remember that and be grateful.

The sun was only just peeking over the horizon, burning off the misty haze of dawn, bathing the orchard in a silvery glow. Dazzling rays of sunlight streaked between the fruit trees, contrasting against the silhouetted branches. Already the morning held promise of another hot September day.

She loved this time of morning, when no one was around, when the rabbits and deer could still be spotted grazing at the windfalls lying in the long grass around the base of the fruit trees.

Whenever she got the opportunity she would hold out an apple to the door, keeping very still, talking softly. Of course they were too jittery to take the fruit, but she held on to the dream that if she was patient enough, one day a deer would venture close enough to eat from her hand.

At least Ted Draper's carthorse had no fear, and she selected a few windfalls and made her way along the pathway that led to the farmer's fields. He would be tending to the sheep at this time of morning. Occasionally their paths crossed, and they'd chat. His wife had died a year or so ago and he'd been left to run the farm and its tied cottage — and bring up four children. Six months ago, he'd suggested they should marry. Although flattered, Lily had let him down as kindly as possible. Nice though he was, she could never marry a man out of convenience.

There was no sign of him this morning, and so she stood on the bottom rung of his fence and whistled. Molly, his carthorse, lumbered over. Apples were a favourite treat, and Lily had bought an apronful.

After fussing the horse, Lily walked on, up the hill to where, on a clear day, you could see three different counties: Sussex, their home county, and glimpses of Hampshire and Surrey in the far distance. Midway were more farms belonging to the estate, each field ripe with corn or barley, or pastureland where flocks of sheep and cattle grazed. Between the fields lay a criss-cross of little pathways flanked by hedgerows that linked the farms and cottages on the Westfall estate.

Lily settled down beneath a massive oak tree — one of her favourite places to sit and read or sketch. She spread out her blanket, eager to begin drawing the wild flowers and fungi growing all around, taking great care to get the smallest of details just *so*.

As she worked, Lily thought about her new book, and the artist who had illustrated it. How wonderful to be employed as an illustrator. In truth, it was something of a pipe dream to find employment as an artist. Who in their right mind would pay good money for her to draw or paint? No, she would go into service, and she would make the move soon. If Prudence and Jude were to start walking out together and eventually marry, it would be intolerable to remain under the same roof and be Prudence's confidante as she gushed on about how much she loved him — and heaven only knew what other intimate secrets she would want to share!

'You do indeed draw remarkably well!'

Lily cried out in fright at the sudden sound of Jude Mitchell's voice close by.

'I'm sorry, I didn't mean to startle you,' he said, crouching down on his haunches next to her. His shirt was open at the throat, with sleeves that were gathered at the wrists. His breeches were stretched taut across powerful thighs. And intense blue eyes were sweeping over her face. There was a softness in the way he regarded her, and an intensity that made her feel that he was searching into her soul.

With a rapidly beating heart she

turned away from him, staring down at her sketchpad. 'Mr Mitchell, you seem to have quite a knack of creeping up behind me.'

'Well, the last time I was behind you, I think you were very much aware of my presence.'

Lily felt her cheeks turning crimson. If he was talking about literally being behind her, on the horse, she had indeed been aware of him — in a very physical sense. Fortunately he didn't wait for her reply.

'Although I don't like to think of myself as creeping,' he said, with laughter in his voice. 'I think it's more of a case of you being so absorbed in your work that you're oblivious to everything else around you — an admirable thing.'

If he expected her to smile back, he was in for a disappointment.

Lily closed her sketchpad and placed her pencils neatly side by side as she turned and glared at him. 'Yes, I was absorbed in my drawing, but you have once again disturbed my peace and solitude. Is there anything I can do for you, or are you just at a loose end waiting for your intended to join you?'

'My what?' His eyebrows arched. 'My intended?'

Lily regarded him questioningly. 'Why should that astonish you? You are Prudence's suitor. It's the reason you're at Westfall Manor, is it not?'

He changed his position to sit on the blanket next to her, and Lily prayed that Prudence wouldn't choose this morning to come spying on her and catch them in another intimate tête-à-tête. She began to pack away her things. No doubt Mrs Pritchard would be making a start on breakfast and be glad of another pair of helping hands.

He, however, seemed to settle down more comfortably. 'Yes, true enough. Initially I came here to meet Prudence, to see how we got along, with a view to marriage. But not everything turns out the way you might expect.'

'It takes time to get to know

someone,' said Lily, on her feet now and indicating that she would like to gather up the blanket he was kneeling on. 'Could I trouble you to move?'

He remained where he was, his expression suddenly downcast. 'Why are you running away from me, Lily? You were quite content sitting sketching before I interrupted you. And if you tell me you have work to do, I'm afraid I won't believe you.'

'It really makes no difference whether you believe me or not, Mr Mitchell . . . '

'Jude,' he reminded her good-humouredly. 'One can hardly remain on formal terms after riding bareback together.'

Lily glared at him. 'It was a horse ride! We were not tucked up in bed together . . . ' She stopped, horrified and embarrassed. Why on earth had she said that?

He, however, seemed to relish the thought. 'Now, there's a thing.'

Her cheeks on fire, she stooped and

tugged at the blanket. 'May I please have my blanket?'

His smile widened, making his eyes sparkle roguishly. 'Forgive me, Lily. I'm merely teasing you.'

'You seem to find great amusement at my cost.'

He got to his feet, allowing her to redeem the blanket. She draped it over her arm and marched back toward the manor house. He followed — or, rather, he strode lazily alongside of her. 'I apologise. It's perhaps because I sense that beneath your austere façade, there's a fun-loving young woman just yearning to run free and wild. Lily, have you ever seen the ocean?'

She momentarily halted in her tracks. She had never thought of herself as austere. Lady Hester was the austere one. If anything, she considered herself . . . reserved, perhaps. And how could she be wild and reckless or frivolous when she had no right to be? She only lived at the manor out of the kindness of the Westfalls' hearts. She had to remain respectful to them. She knew her place . . . She halted this train of thought. No, she didn't know her place. She had no place. She belonged nowhere. Her thoughts plummeted.

'Lily?'

She couldn't think straight. Jude Mitchell was quite unsettling. 'Mr Mitchell, I don't know why you are plaguing me like this. Maybe it's some kind of sport to you, but . . . '

'Don't you, Lily?' he asked, stepping directly in front of her, blocking her escape. He looked into her eyes, sending her heart racing. 'Don't you?'

She felt breathless. 'Would you kindly let me pass?'

'Of course,' he said, hesitating just for a second before moving aside. 'Forgive me, I'm an idiot!'

Lily swept by him and marched back towards the manor. She had gone twenty steps before she realised that he wasn't keeping pace with her now. She glanced back over her shoulder and saw that he was still standing there, his head lowered.

'Yes, hang your head in shame, Jude Mitchell,' Lily muttered under her breath. He was here for Prudence, yet flirting outrageously with her. He wasn't being fair to either of them. She quickened her step, eager to get well away from Jude Mitchell and the cruel game he was playing.

Arriving back in the kitchen, Mrs Pritchard was turning out delicious-smelling kedgeree into a china serving dish while Dorothy was making a pot of tea. It was the usual routine at breakfast time. The family, and any guests who happened to be staying, would have the smoky fish-and-rice dish, or poached eggs, or bacon. The staff and Lily would eat later.

Covering the large teapot with a knitted cosy, Dorothy glanced at Lily and grinned. 'He's awfully handsome, don't you think, Lily?'

Lily groaned inwardly. There was just no getting away from the man. 'Yes, I suppose he is.'

'Miss Prudence won't be turning her nose up at this one, I'll be bound.'

'Dorothy!' Mrs Pritchard chided, giving the young maid one of her sterner glares, which were nowhere near as withering as Hester's black looks.

Dorothy merely chuckled. 'Mrs Pritchard, you wait till you see him. He'd even turn your head. He's tall, isn't he, Lily? I think Mrs Pritchard could easily stand under his armpit.'

'As if I'd be doing that!' the cook dismissed, her cheeks turning pink now. 'And if that tea is brewed, I suggest you take it through to the dining room, then hurry back for this kedgeree. You know, your trouble, young lady, is that you spend too long chattering. It's not your place to go making comments about guests and family matters. Irreverent babble leads to ungodliness. Now, you think on that, young lady!'

'Yes, Mrs Pritchard,' Dorothy said with a cheeky grin.

The cook smiled at Lily. 'Make yourself some breakfast, dear. There's eggs and bacon. I'll see to Dorothy's and mine in a little while, once the family are sorted.'

Lily was quite hungry, and so she cooked herself some food and did her best to chat about normal things — things that didn't revolve around Jude Mitchell. Although she was beginning to realise that was a total impossibility. It seemed that everything was revolving around Jude Mitchell at the moment.

8

'Fool!' Jude muttered under his breath as Lily stormed angrily away from him. He couldn't blame her. He was acting like a complete idiot, or like some sexual predator. She wasn't used to such attention from a man. She really was as sweet and innocent as she looked.

He kicked at the ground, angry with himself. She honestly couldn't see that he was attracted to her. It was quite simply black and white with her. In Lily's eyes, he was here courting Prudence, so he shouldn't be lavishing his time and attention on her.

But he couldn't help himself. He was totally smitten with Lily Baines. And now he was in a very awkward position. It was wrong to remain here, accepting the Westfalls' hospitality, under the pretence of getting to know Prudence.

He already knew as much as he wanted to know about her. There would be no marriage between them, and would not have been even if he hadn't set eyes on Lily.

However, the fact was, he *had* met Lily, and he wanted to know more about her. He wanted to spend every waking minute getting to know her. But he was messing everything up. Living as a widower these last few years, he was ridiculously out of practice in knowing how to deal with this sort of situation — knowing how to show a woman that he liked and respected her. He was behaving like a complete idiot. And, rather than making her warm to him, everything he said or did was driving the wedge between them ever deeper.

He ought to leave Sir Joseph's home. It wasn't right to lead Prudence on. But to leave so soon meant leaving Lily too. And he could not bring himself to do that.

Returning to the house, wondering

whether Lily would be serving breakfast, Jude bumped into Sir Joseph in the hallway. The older man's face lit up on seeing him.

'Jude! Good morning. I trust you slept soundly.'

'Indeed I did,' he answered, knowing it to be a lie. He'd actually lain awake half the night thinking about Lily Baines. She was like a breath of fresh air that had blown into his life — even though most of the time she gave him short shrift. But he was positive that her outer façade was a shell that she surrounded herself with. One he was desperate to break through, although his attempts so far were pretty pathetic.

Sir Joseph patted his back, like a man might show affection to his future son-in-law. To Jude, it almost felt like a noose tightening around his neck.

'A good hearty breakfast, and then I thought we might all take a stroll around the estate,' said Sir Joseph. 'You'll be interested in the various cottage industries we have going on.

We're quite the hive of industry, you know!'

'That sounds excellent,' said Jude, easing his conscience by deciding it was an opportunity to see if anyone was producing something that could be exported overseas, and hence strike up some sort of business deal.

Sir Joseph led the way into the dining room. 'First, though, we need to tuck into Mrs Pritchard's kedgeree before it goes cold, or I fear we shall be in her bad books.'

Hester and Prudence were already seated at the table. There was a place set for him beside Prudence; he was relieved to see she was dressed more demurely this morning and he wasn't faced with a heaving bare bosom over breakfast. Both women smiled as he entered.

Taking a deep breath, he pushed aside all thoughts of Lily and bowed his head courteously to his hosts. 'Good morning, ladies. I apologise if I have kept you waiting.'

Prudence patted the chair next to her. 'Sit here beside me, Jude. Dorothy will serve breakfast and afterwards we're going to show you around our land. You'll be astonished at how big the Westfall estate is. Papa says I'll be a very wealthy landowner myself one day. I can hardly wait!'

Jude sat down, aware that his chair was just a little too close to Prudence's, and guessing that she had pulled it nearer deliberately. It would be churlish to adjust it, so he sat elbow-to-elbow with her, listening with apparent rapture to her relentless, pointless chatter,

He was aware that Lady Hester, seated opposite, was observing his every move. No doubt she had more brains than her pretty daughter. And he had the distinct feeling that she could be devious if she wanted to be. Well, it wasn't going to happen. There would be no marriage between him and Prudence. Lord, he would rather cut off his own foot!

After she had eaten breakfast, Lily decided to go out into the vegetable garden and pick peas for the evening meal. As she plucked the fresh green peapods from their stalks, she tried not to think about what Jude had implied. *Not everything turns out the way you might expect.* Was he saying that he wasn't interested in Prudence — that he was interested in her?

It was ridiculous, and she refused to even think of such a thing. He was dallying with her. Clearly he was the sort of man who wanted a wife *and* a mistress. Well, she was not going to be the other woman in his life!

Prudence really did need to know the sort of man she was getting mixed up with. Although she would not take kindly to being told.

With her bowl brimming with peapods, Lily glanced across the gardens to see the family strolling around the side of the manor house, taking the morning air.

Jude was walking alongside Prudence with her parents just a few steps behind. They hadn't seen her. The early-morning sun was at the back of her, and she was half-hidden behind the tall trellised rows of peas and beans. She could hear Prudence's excited chatter, and as Lily stood watching, she couldn't help but notice how she constantly touched Jude's arm as they strolled along the path, and how he inclined his head towards her, clearly fascinated by her conversation and no doubt quite taken with her charms.

There was a dull ache in Lily's breast. A dreadful sadness creeping through her that she wished with all her heart she could shake off. But they looked so right together, a happy family gathering, four wealthy people of equal class and standing: Prudence, a beautiful and eligible young woman — and Jude, an eligible widower looking for a wife. A sob caught in her throat, and she wished with all her heart that she had never set eyes on Jude Mitchell.

She couldn't bear to stand here watching them any longer. Head down, she hurried back towards the kitchen.

'Lily!'

She heard Prudence's shout but ignored it. Perhaps she had forgotten her bossiness yesterday, but Lily certainly had not.

'Lily!' It was Sir Joseph calling her now.

She stopped. She had the greatest respect for him and couldn't deliberately ignore him. Both Sir Joseph and Prudence were beckoning for her to join them.

She had no option. It wasn't as if she had to get indoors and do her chores. She didn't have any chores — and again, that bothered her immensely. This situation could not go on. She needed proper employment. She needed to take control of her life.

Breathing rapidly, Lily tried to compose herself. Somehow she had to put on an act. To pretend there was nothing wrong, and that she wasn't envious of Prudence. And, most importantly, to show Jude Mitchell that she wasn't in the slightest bit interested in him.

Prudence broke free of the group and, holding up the hem of her gown, came dashing towards her. 'Lily!'

She waited for Prudence to reach her, aware that Jude was standing a little apart from Sir Joseph and Lady Hester, as if he'd gone to chase after his bride-to-be. Perhaps he was afraid that Lily would tell Prudence what he'd said earlier. She looked away from them all, wishing she could just escape.

'Lily, I'm so glad I've caught you,' Prudence said breathlessly. 'I wanted to say sorry. You know, for being such a bossy-boots yesterday. I have to admit, I was a bit jealous that you'd got your hands on Jude before I had. Do you forgive me?'

Lily bit hard on her lip, hoping to mask her true feelings. 'Of course. It was my fault. I should have mentioned it earlier.'

'So you aren't cross with me?'

Lily managed a smile. Prudence looked so happy, so excited. Desperately, she tried not to envy her. 'No, of course not.'

Prudence hugged her. 'Come and join us, Lily. We're showing Jude around the estate.'

Lily glanced over to the waiting threesome. Jude was staring this way, his shoulders set squarely, looking tense. And well he might, Lily thought. She smiled at Prudence. 'That's very kind of you, but I have something important to do.'

Prudence thought that hilarious and gave a little squeal of laughter. 'Oh Lily, what could possibly be important? Do you have to read another chapter of some boring book? Or paint another flower in your sketchpad?'

Lily tried hard not to let Prudence's mockery upset her. It was just her way. But it deepened her resolve to find a proper career for herself. There was no reason she couldn't find a housekeeping job somewhere. Surely Mrs Pritchard would help her find suitable employment. 'Actually, I have to speak to the cook . . .'

'Oh, well, if you're going to bake a cake, that *is* important,' laughed Prudence. 'But could you please, please, please make the walnut cake? That is so scrumptious!'

'That wasn't what I intended seeing her about, actually,' said Lily, feeling a tightness in her chest — a feeling that things *had* to change. She just couldn't remain being this burden to the family. She was eighteen, she needed proper employment — a reason for being here on this earth — now more so than ever. If Prudence and Jude were to marry, she would have to endure these awful, painful feelings forever. The prospect of that was intolerable. She forced a smile. 'Enjoy your walk, Prudence.'

Prudence lowered her voice. 'I'll see you later, Lily — and who knows, I may have something exciting to tell you!'

'Yes, who knows?' agreed Lily, turning, deliberately not glancing towards the rest of the family or Jude — particularly not Jude.

She hurried towards the house, her head erect, eyes focused straight ahead; positive they were all watching after her. The house had never seemed so far away.

★   ★   ★

Had it not been for the tenants around the Westfall farmlands involved in so many different crafts and skills, Jude would have exploded with frustration as they toured the huge estate.

Perhaps if he had just been with Sir Joseph, things might have been more tolerable; but with the wife and daughter in tow, the man's conversation was governed and guided by them. Sir Joseph was subdued when talking about his own work and interests, and only became animated when he was gushing about his silly daughter and vowing what a wonderful wife she would make.

Out of devilment and boredom, Jude decided to take them up on such a possibility. They had stopped at one of the cottages where the tenants kept sheep and spun wool which the women of the house knitted into garments. The grandmother of the family provided tea, bread and cheese for them, and then returned to her spinning, leaving her landlords to relax in privacy.

'What do you like to cook, Prudence?' Jude asked, gazing deliberately across the small scrubbed table to look into her eyes, secretly searching for a glint of substance there. 'Do you bake puddings? I have a very sweet tooth. Or do you excel in making stews and soups? My appetite is enormous.'

Hester made a funny little coughing sound and gave her daughter a wide-eyed look that told her to answer sensibly. Jude pretended he hadn't noticed the prompt.

'Oh, well, cooking isn't exactly my

forte,' Prudence had the grace to admit. 'Mrs Pritchard is such a wonderful cook I've never . . . '

'So you don't cook,' Jude remarked, raising his eyebrows to indicate that she had failed question number one. He posed another question. 'I imagine that, being the future landowner, you help your parents with the accounts: Making sure the rents and income from your tenants are collected on time, that sort of thing.'

She shot a desperate glance at her father, who answered for her.

'We are currently exploring those avenues,' said Sir Joseph. 'Prudence has a lot to learn, but we are making great progress. She has a very smart head on her shoulders . . . '

'As well as it being a very pretty head,' Jude finished for him, realising that her charms were indeed all that she had going for her.

Hester who hadn't touched her tea or the food, did her best not to sound like a shrew when she said, 'Our daughter is a respectable young lady. We employ people to undertake such humdrum work as cooking and accountancy. Her role would be to provide a happy home for her husband, and not to be too exhausted at the end of the day to attend to his needs.'

'Indeed,' Jude acknowledged, bowing his head graciously. 'Companionship is something a man needs and desires. But Prudence, how would you feel being left alone for weeks, maybe months, should a husband have to travel away with his work? How would you fill your days?'

'Well, should I be in London, where my husband's work was, there would be plenty to do every day,' Prudence said, doing her best to answer his hypothetical question. 'I would shop for the latest fashions, to make sure I looked my very best when he came home. And I'm sure I should get involved in society, and make some friends with whom I could lunch and hold soirées.'

Jude saw the expressions on both Sir

Joseph and Hester's faces. He didn't have to wait long before they both chipped in with suggestions of how she *would* pass her days, which Prudence declared she was just about to say.

If it wasn't so pathetic, Jude would have laughed, but thoughts of Isabella were running through his head. What a woman she had been. Never afraid to get her hands dirty, knowing all about his cargo business: keeping the books, involving herself with his employee's families; making sure there were no problems when the men were away at sea. She even involved herself in charitable work, trying to get the street girls into proper employment. At times she worked herself too hard. Tragically, she had worked herself into the ground when he had been away on a month-long voyage. Her body must have been at a very low ebb that winter when she'd caught influenza. She hadn't taken enough care of herself, continuing to go helping others. The influenza had turned into pneumonia.

He had arrived home just in time for her to die in his arms.

'We'll move on, shall we, Jude?' Sir Joseph's voice cut through his bleak thoughts.

He rallied and got to his feet, holding the chair for Hester. 'We must thank the family for their hospitality.' He didn't wait for anyone to agree or disagree, but strode through to the back room, where they were working on their spinning wheels.

He placed a half-crown on a shelf. 'Thank you for your kindness.'

'Not at all, sir . . . ' began the grandmother. Nevertheless, her wrinkled face lit up as she saw the silver coin.

'Your hospitality is very much appreciated,' Jude dismissed as he went outside, where the family were waiting and eager to show him more of their assets. For a while he felt like a donkey with carrots dangling under his nose.

★   ★   ★

'There!' said Mrs Pritchard, finally closing the big ledger of household accounts 'I think you've studied enough for one day, Lily. Besides I have dinner to prepare.'

Lily got to her feet and stretched. She had been sitting at the kitchen table for the last three hours as Mrs Pritchard patiently explained how a housekeeper kept her books and worked out how much produce a house needed, dependant upon the number of people it had to cater for and all sorts of other factors, even regarding what time of year it was.

'It's fascinating!' Lily declared. 'I hadn't realised there was so much to think about. Let me help you with dinner now. I'll make the pastry for the rabbit pie if you like.'

The cook took a long, thoughtful look at Lily, and then smiled. 'You're so like your mother, it's uncanny. She was a good worker too. You know something, Lily, I'm ever so glad you're thinking about going into service to earn your living. It's all very well living here under this grand roof, but that's not doing you any good in the long run.'

'I know that,' Lily acknowledged. 'I feel like I've wasted too many years already.'

'Now, don't you be thinking that,' Mrs Pritchard admonished. 'It's not like you've been sitting idle on your backside. You've always helped me, and you've been giving yourself a good education, reading like you do. Mind you, I can't help wondering whether going into service is your best choice. You could get a job in an office or anywhere if you put your mind to it. And your drawings and paintings are a treat. Could you not find work putting your artistic talents to good use? Newspapers have advertisements in them, and someone has to draw them.'

'That would be a dream come true, Mrs Pritchard. Do you really think I might try for such a position?'

'You're as intelligent as the next

person, Lily. If I was you, I'd ask Sir Joseph for a bit of advice when he's got a minute.'

Lily felt a little surge of excitement, and for the first time that day, found that she was daydreaming about a career — instead of daydreaming about Jude Mitchell.

After making the pastry for the pie, Lily spent some time in the library. She sat at the stately mahogany bureau near the window, browsing through an encyclopaedia, admiring the drawings and pondering seriously about how one could get employment as an illustrator. Eventually, footfalls in the hall and Prudence's excitable chatter drifting along the corridor told her they were back.

Determinedly, she refused to let the proximity of Jude Mitchell dampen her enthusiasm for a career. Her talk with Mrs Pritchard had set her hopes soaring. Perhaps she could find work with a publishing house. She had no idea how to go about such a thing.

When Sir Joseph wasn't so busy with his guest, she would speak to him, and hope he didn't think she was acting above her station. Right now, however, he was preoccupied with securing Jude Mitchell as his future son-in-law.

The thought sent a shaft of pain through her heart, and she tried her hardest not to dwell on it. She had better things to think about. And when the library door opened a short while later and she assumed it was Sir Joseph, she impulsively began to blurt out her question.

'Sir Joseph, could I ask you . . . ' Looking up, she saw it wasn't Sir Joseph at all. Her insides somersaulted. 'Jude!'

He closed the library door behind him and leant against it, almost as if the breath had been knocked out of him. 'Lily.'

Her heart began to race. All her good intentions of not thinking about him flew out the window. 'Have . . . have you had an enjoyable day? I'm glad the weather stayed fine for your tour of the estate; when it rains it can be quite marshy in pl — -'

He crossed the room in two strides and stood towering over her, his features set like granite. 'No, Lily, I have not had a good day.'

'I'm sorry to hear that.' She frowned, not sure whether his mood was due to anything she had done. 'You didn't enjoy spending the day with Prudence?'

He ran his fingers through his hair as if exasperated. 'Prudence is as pretty as a mannequin in a fashion-store window, and with about as much sense and personality!'

'Don't!' Lily gasped, confused by his mood and attitude. 'I'm sure she would be terribly hurt to hear you talk about her in such a way.'

'No doubt,' he sighed. 'But the reason I have not had a good day, Lily, is because I haven't been able to get you out of my mind.'

Her violet eyes widened in alarm. 'Why? What have I done?'

He heaved a long-drawn-out breath, and his eyes lifted towards the heavens for a second. 'Lily Baines, I'll tell you what you've done. You have bewitched me, robbed me of my senses.'

She looked at him, horrified. 'I'm sure I've done no such thing!'

'Yes, you have, Lily,' he said tenderly, taking her hands and drawing her to her feet. 'You're on my mind constantly. I can't sleep . . . do you know the willpower I needed last night not to come knocking at your bedroom door?'

'Stop it!' Lily cried, pulling her hands free, turning away. But it shocked her to think he'd been longing for her, just as she'd been wanting him. To think that she'd been on the brink of leaving her bedroom last night, to accidentally-on-purpose bump into him.

She thanked her good senses that she hadn't. This man needed no encouragement. And already she felt that she was in far deeper than she could handle. No doubt if she was to give him an inch he would take a mile. But, of course, on the other hand he was probably lying. He was a womaniser. Clearly, courting Prudence wasn't sufficient for him. He obviously thought it good sport to bag two females for the price of one.

Yet the way he was looking at her, with such anguish, made her wonder. She was not about to crumble, however. She took a steadying breath. 'Mr Mitchell, you should not be speaking to me in this manner.'

'You called me Jude a moment ago, when you were startled,' he said, looking utterly forlorn. 'Before you had the chance to draw up that protective armour you surround yourself with. But no, no doubt I shouldn't be speaking in this way to you. Yet I must. I'll be leaving here soon. I can't continue accepting the family's hospitality when there will be no union between Prudence and I.'

She stared at him. He looked and sounded sincere, yet she had no experience of men and their lies. 'Have you told Prudence this? Or her family?'

'Not yet. As soon as I do, I'll undoubtedly be shown the door. And I needed to talk to you, Lily, to let you know of my feelings towards you. To ask if you'd allow me to write to you when I'm gone from here. Perhaps we could arrange to meet up in London, or I'll come here when I can, see if I can find lodgings in the village. So we can get to know one another.'

She felt hot, and her heart was racing. 'Mr Mitchell, all this talk is making me giddy. I've seen you with Prudence, hanging on her every word. You looked extremely enamoured with her.'

He shook his head. 'Merely politeness and courtesy. I've no wish to hurt the girl.'

'So you feign interest. You put on an act,' Lily accused.

'Yes, in a way . . . '

'So how am I to know you aren't play-acting now?' she angrily demanded. 'How do I know this isn't some sport, some game you're playing?'

'Lily, there has been too much sorrow in my life to be a philanderer. When my wife died, I never thought I'd meet another woman who I wanted to spend my days with. But then you came along, and you've stolen my heart.'

'I'm sure I've done no such thing,' she repeated, but deep inside she felt a little surge of hope. Was it possible that he was telling her the truth? Dared she drop her guard and allow him into her life? She rallied against her weakening resolve. She really ought to trust her first instincts — that he was a flirt and womaniser.

'Yes you have, Lily,' he said softly, moving closer, taking her hands in his, bringing them to his lips. Planting light kisses on the palms of her hands with every word he spoke. 'You have bewitched me, Lily.'

His kisses against the soft flesh of her palms sent tremors of delight through her body. It was impossible to pull away, even if she'd wanted to. There was some invisible tether binding her to him, leaving her wanting more of his kisses, more of his sweet talk, more of those sensual looks that bore right through to her inner core.

'And I can see in your beautiful eyes, Lily, that you want me too.'

'I do not!' she cried, burning with shame that she'd allowed his kisses to charm her. She pulled free from his hold, tried to put distance between them. But his arm snaked around her waist, drawing her back to him, so that her body was pressed against his. One hand remained on the small of her back, the other cupped the nape of her neck as his lips found hers.

For a moment she struggled, but the touch of his mouth on hers sent stars exploding in her head and tremors of desire tingling through her veins. It was the most natural thing in the world to kiss him in return, to press closer to him and feel the powerful strength of his ruggedly hard torso.

She felt his passion rising, and gasped as his kiss deepened and his arms tightened, his hands stroking and caressing. It was as if he had unleashed the woman in her. Never had she felt such desire, such longing to be in a man's arms — in his bed. He moaned her name, quickening her pulse. Her need for him was overwhelming. It was madness, she knew it was madness. But she was beyond caring — beyond being rational.

The strength of her feelings frightened her suddenly. She wanted nothing more than to give away her innocence to this man. A man she barely knew. Good sense began to creep back into her consciousness. Right from the start, she had thought him to be a womaniser, a seducer — and he was clearly an expert at his art.

She drew back from him breathlessly. 'We have to stop this . . . '

'No, Lily. This is just the start. We must make plans.'

Lily marvelled as she saw the love shining from his blue eyes. Surely he couldn't feign such a physical reaction.

Unless it wasn't love at all — but lust. She needed time, she needed space to get things into proportion. To do nothing until she was positive that she could trust him. She needed to be sure there was no relationship between him and Prudence. She would never intentionally hurt her dear friend. And it was clear that Prudence was smitten with Jude. Unless, of course, he was lying, and this was his normal behaviour — seducing every woman he came into contact with.

'I have to go,' Lily said, pulling free from his embrace.

'Lily. We must talk, tomorrow — at daybreak. I'll see you by the oak tree, where you were this morning.'

'I don't know . . . '

The library door opened suddenly, and Lady Hester appeared, already catching the last of the conversation. 'What don't you know?' she demanded, narrowing her eyes.

Lily felt a wave of sickness rush over her. Thank heavens that Hester hadn't come in just a few seconds earlier. That would indeed have been disastrous. The woman was regarding her suspiciously, waiting for an answer.

'I don't know if Sir Joseph has any books on sea voyages,' she answered, her eyes flashing unspoken messages at Jude. She continued walking, browsing the shelves as if assisting Jude on his quest for novels on sea voyages. She had no idea how she'd come up with that. 'Let me see . . . ' she mused.

'You do a lot of reading, then, Mr Mitchell?' asked Lady Hester, giving him no chance to reply as she continued sharply, 'I had no idea. I think Lily knows more about you then the rest of us put together! Shall we go in to dinner — unless you'd like to stay here with Lily and discuss literature?'

Lily could scarcely breathe. If he'd actually meant what he'd just said to her, he could at any second inform Lady Hester that she was not about to become his mother-in-law. Lily held her breath, waiting for the damning words that would turn the Westfalls against her forever. Even if he didn't drag her into his decision, Lily had no doubt that the blame would be laid squarely on her shoulders.

For what seemed an eternity, yet was probably only a second or two, Jude stood silently, his eyes boring into the back of Lily's head as she pretended to be searching for a particular book. Then, to her relief, he spoke, his voice perfectly under control.

'My apologies if I've kept you all waiting. Books are a passion of mine — one of my passions.'

Lily's eyes fluttered shut, knowing full well that another of his passions was making love.

Hester linked his arm. 'Well, I hope you don't mind being dragged away to eat dinner. We have shoulder of lamb. It's quite succulent.'

'Wonderful! I'm ravenous,' he said, catching Lily's eye in a way that said his hunger was not for food. 'I can't remember when I was more ravenous.'

She could scarcely breathe as Hester escorted him from the library, her head tilted in such a way as to remind Lily of her place. And that Jude was here for her daughter — not for her. Lily sensed that if Jude *was* telling the truth, and he curtailed his budding relationship with Prudence, Lady Hester would be furious.

As the library door closed behind them, Lily tried to calm her breathing. Although, after what had just happened, she feared she would never breathe normally ever again.

9

Lily lay in bed, staring out at the moon and stars as her fingers touched the precious cross around her throat, wishing she was not so alone in this world. Wishing for someone she could talk to, share her thoughts and worries with, ask guidance from.

But there was no one. She had to make her own decisions. And the biggest decision at the moment was whether to meet Jude at daybreak or not.

Was Jude serious or just playing games with her emotions? Would he really turn Prudence down in favour of her? It seemed most unlikely. Yet if it proved to be true, if tomorrow Jude Mitchell left and returned home, leaving Prudence behind, then she would forever bitterly regret not having the courage to meet him and discover the real man.

It was impossible to settle to her reading, and so she began sketching. There was only one image in her mind. It was so easy to capture that physique, that stance, the style of clothing. Closing her eyes, she pictured his face — that angular bone structure, the straight nose, the intensity of his gaze, and those lips. Her pencil skimmed lightly over the paper, softly smudging the lines to create a softness to his mouth . . .

The memory of his kiss sent tingles through her body. Suddenly she knew that, come the morning, she would throw caution to the wind and meet him.

Lily sketched until her candles had burned low. Finally she put away her pad and pencils, blew out the candles, and rested her head on her pillow. She was almost asleep when she heard a soft footfall outside her room. Her heart leapt as a light knock sounded on her door and she heard Jude speak her name.

'Lily?'

She lay motionless, eyes wide, breath locked in her breast, every fibre of her being crying out to open her door — and her heart — to him. She sensed his presence, so close . . . but there was no other sound until moments later she heard his bedroom door open and close. Lily lay perfectly still, listening to her thudding heartbeat until finally she slept.

The sun was just rising when she awoke. She washed, dressed, and brushed the tangles from her hair, trying not to think about Jude. She was simply going for an early-morning walk as normal. There was no reason to feel guilty — or excited. Yet she did. Her heart was racing and her cheeks were flushed; catching sight of her reflection in the small mirror, there was no hiding the sparkle in her eyes.

Jude probably wouldn't even be there, she warned herself. He had probably knocked at her door last night to say he had changed his mind. Well, it mattered not a jot. She intended enjoying the beautiful morning. In fact, she preferred to be alone so she could concentrate on her art.

Taking a small blanket to sit on, Lily went softly from her room. It was impossible not to glance across the corridor to his bedroom. Was he still asleep? Or already at their meeting place by the oak?

Most likely fast asleep. In fact, she fervently hoped he was still asleep. And as she tiptoed downstairs she told herself the lightness of her step was so as not to waken him.

It was another glorious morning. A misty haze smothered the lawns and fields, making it look as if the trees were standing in a cloud. Blackbirds chirruped to one another as if in conversation as she made her way to the oak. She walked on, seeing no one, plucking an apple from a tree for breakfast. Nearing the oak tree, her heartbeat quickened. Just as swiftly, it lurched. The tree stood lonely in the cloud of mist. No handsome buccaneer leaning against its solid trunk awaiting her arrival. Her heart plummeted. So he was still in bed, sound asleep, dreaming no doubt about Prudence.

Lily felt so foolish suddenly, and angry. Why had she been so gullible to have actually believed him? And why venture out so early? She must look so eager — not that he was here to see her.

She instantly wanted to turn tail and go back to the house. She was a fool. He was a womaniser and simply stringing her along.

She strengthened her resolve. She wasn't here for Jude Mitchell's benefit. She was up early to sketch, even though the meadow flowers were still cloaked in early-morning mist. No matter, she told herself, spreading out the blanket. She would sit and relax, breathe in the sweet air, and eat her apple.

She did just that, and there was still no sign of him by the time she had finished it. Angry with herself for not ridding him from her mind, she opened her sketchpad. With a groan of misery, it opened to the sketch she'd done of him.

'You've drawn me!'

His voice made her cry out in surprise. Instantly her heart leapt with joy, but she quickly hid her delight. Instead, she flashed angry eyes his way. 'Must you always sneak up on me? I swear I would have a bell tied around your neck, as you'd do with a kitten.'

'Believe me, Lily Baines,' he said, sitting down beside her, 'I am no kitten!'

She averted her eyes, unwilling to meet his smouldering gaze. The way he'd looked at her yesterday as Hester had escorted him from the library was imprinted on her mind. It was a look that burned with desire. Alone now with him, she doubted she could handle such blatant sexuality.

She turned the pages of her sketchpad, to some half-finished drawings of violets. But he was so close she could smell the fresh male muskiness of the man.

He reached over and turned the page back. 'You've been very kind to me, Lily. I feel flattered.'

She didn't know how to respond. To say she hadn't meant to flatter him, this was just how he looked, would indicate that she found him attractive. But to say that yes he should feel flattered might suggest she'd taken time to make him look so handsome. And so she said nothing, and turned to a clean page.

'Did you sleep well last night, Lily?'

'Yes, why shouldn't I?'

'You didn't hear me knocking at your door, whispering your name?'

A moment of hesitation might have given him a truthful answer, but she responded, 'I told you, I slept soundly.'

His voice was throaty. 'Lily Baines, what are you doing to me? I can't sleep. You're on my mind from morning till night.'

She longed to tell him that she felt the same, but she held back, keeping her feelings locked secretly inside. Blandly, she said, 'Well, here I am, Mr Mitchell . . . '

'Jude. Lily, won't you drop the barrier enough to call me by my Christian name?'

'Jude,' she relented, daring to look into his eyes, searching those deep blue pools to see whether he was genuine or this was all part of his act. What she felt and saw made her heart lurch. He was looking at her with love — and with passion, as if he wanted to sweep her up into his arms and make love to her forever. She turned away. 'Don't look at me like that!'

'Lily,' he murmured, taking her hands in his. 'You need to know, Lily, that I think . . . I am falling in love with you.'

His words shocked her. 'You barely know me!'

'I know. And isn't that the most wondrous thing — to feel so enraptured, so passionate about you after such a short time? Lily, just think how our passion will grow as we discover each other. As we peel away the layers and see each other as we truly are.'

She wanted to believe him. Wished she could be certain. 'Please, you must not speak to me in this manner. You are here for Prudence . . . '

'Prudence means nothing to me, Lily. Even if I had never set eyes upon you, there would be no relationship between her and I.' Tiny creases formed around his eyes as if painful memories were clouding his vision. 'Lily, I was married to a wonderful, intelligent, compassionate woman. I could never be attracted to someone as frivolous and selfish as Prudence. But you, Lily Baines, make life worth living again.'

'Do I?' she murmured, desperately wanting to trust him. 'Then tell me about your life. I know nothing of you.'

His frown lifted, but his gaze was locked on to her face. 'My life is full: full of ships and produce — tea, coffee, spices, all kinds of goods from far-off countries. It's full of seafaring men who rely on me to put money in their pockets so they can feed their families. Lily, too much of my life is spent on the high seas; but as there's no one at home for me, where else would I be?'

'Did your wife . . . ' She hesitated, wondering if he would supply her name.

'Isabella,' he answered, picking up on her unspoken question.

'Did Isabella mind being left alone while you were at sea?'

'I like to think that she missed me,' he said wistfully. 'But she was very much into social reform. She was passionate about helping the poor and needy. She would try and find proper work for the street girls. She and my mother were kept very busy in the poor districts of London.'

Lily was enraptured by his voice. It was mellow, and she sensed he spoke from the heart. Her opinion of him being a shallow womaniser was diminishing rapidly. 'That is most admirable. But wasn't she lonely without you?'

'After my father died, my mother came to live with us. My wife and my mother became good friends. I have a house — I don't live permanently on board a ship!' His face broke into a smile. 'Should I ever be fortunate enough to have a wife again, I would ensure she wasn't lonely, or left alone for too long. But the sea is in my blood. I hope she would understand that.'

Lily tried to imagine life on the open seas. The prospect of painting such scenes excited her. 'Couldn't your wife accompany you on your voyages?'

His eyebrows rose, as if the idea had never occurred to him. 'I can't imagine any woman wanting to! It's bitterly cold and you get soaked to the skin, living quarters are far from luxurious, and it's extremely dangerous. My father died trying to rescue a crewman who had fallen overboard.'

Lily saw the pain in his eyes and instinctively touched his hand. 'I'm sorry to hear that.'

His hand covered hers, holding it in

place, as if that was where it belonged. 'You have a kind heart, Lily. I knew it from the moment I set eyes on you.'

Inwardly her happiness soared. 'I think I was a little sharp with you.'

'No doubt I deserved it!'

'Indeed you did,' she retorted, casting him a serious frown. 'I found you most forward in your approach.'

'You'd knocked me for six, Lily. The moment I set eyes on you, I was smitten.' He moved even closer. 'I *am* smitten, Lily. You are beautiful, and I long to kiss you again . . . '

She longed for that kiss too, but she battled against falling into his arms. 'Jude, you know so little about me. You might discover that I am vain, or dull, or bad-tempered. I might be a shrew for all you know.'

'Even if you were all those things, I would still want you beside me, close to me. And I'd still want you to love me.'

Stunned, Lily could only stare at him, her heart thudding inside her ribcage, a fierce need rising to feel his arms around her. Feel his lips on hers. 'Kiss me then, Jude,' she breathed, hearing the words and amazed that she had uttered them.

With eyes half-closed his lips brushed lightly against hers. Instinctively, Lily's arms slid around his neck, her fingers tangling into his dark hair. Her eyelids fluttered as a million stars exploded in her head.

His kiss deepened and she welcomed it, welcomed the feel of his strong arms around her, sensuous hands caressing her, sending shivers racing through her body.

Slowly, he eased her backwards until she was lying on the blanket, his powerful body half-covering hers, his hand now stroking the swell of her breast. She arched into him, some carnal instinct within breaking free, unleashing her desires. She ached to know the intimacy of making love with Jude.

She murmured his name against his lips, and his kisses became more urgent, more demanding. Then, with a groan, he eased himself away from her.

'Lily,' he breathed, 'you are the most wonderful, beautiful woman, and I swear I am struggling with all my heart not to make love to you right here and now.'

'But I want you, Jude,' she murmured, her throat aching with longing.

Leaning on one elbow to gaze down into her flushed face, he said, 'I will put a ring on your finger first, my sweet.'

Lily was tingling with desire, and his words caused her emotions to collide — joy and disappointment. Thrilled that he should want to marry her — agonised to physically want him so badly and know it was not to be, at least for a while.

But he had proved himself not to be a philanderer. A womaniser would surely have jumped at the opportunity of making love to her. Now, as the moment passed, it shocked her to realise how abandoned she had been.

She sat up, her cheeks flushed. He

was looking at her with love shining from his eyes.

'You are truly beautiful,' he said, picking a blade of grass from her hair. 'Lily, I never thought I would meet another woman who could make me feel so alive. Made me realise that life is worth living after all.'

'You'd had such thoughts? When your wife died?'

He nodded. 'I kept going for the sake of the men who work for me. The responsibility of the company had fallen on my shoulders when my father died, not long before losing Isabella.'

Lily took his hand, wanting to know everything about this man — this man that she had fallen so deeply in love with. 'What tragedies you've suffered.'

His eyes shone with love. 'Yes, but I have found you, Lily Baines. Tell me about yourself. Your life has clearly not been easy, losing your parents so young. I want to know everything about you — will you tell me of your life, Lily?'

'Yes,' she promised, certain that he

would not be judgemental against her unmarried mother. Trusting him as she had never trusted anyone before.

10

Jude had never felt happier as he walked back to the manor house hand-in-hand with Lily. She'd been reluctant to begin with to talk about her mother being unmarried, but he'd slowly gained her trust. He'd learnt that she had never known her father, and that the Westfalls had provided a home for her out of the kindness of their hearts.

Recalling how he had mistaken her for Sir Joseph's daughter, it occurred to him that perhaps she *did* know her father without realising it. He kept his thoughts to himself and listened without comment, except to reassure her that her mother was undoubtedly a good woman.

As the manor house came into view, Lily released his hand. For a moment he had felt quite bereft, but of course it was the sensible thing to do. Lily still had to live and work here. Perhaps, though, soon he could make plans for them to be together. The thought made him ridiculously excited, like some teenage boy with his first love. Close to the house, they parted with the promise of meeting again at daybreak.

Now, he had to prepare himself to thank the Westfalls for their hospitality, and to leave. He dreaded having to tell Prudence that their relationship would be going no further. He doubted she would take the news graciously. But under no circumstances would he draw Lily into this.

Sir Joseph, Lady Hester and Prudence were just settling themselves at the breakfast table, and he marvelled at his own good timing. Prudence looked as pretty as ever, although her gown was far too low with an abundance of cleavage on show. His thoughts drifted longingly back to the soft curves of Lily's body and he sighed.

'We're going for a picnic this

afternoon,' Prudence declared, leaning towards him.

'That's if Mr Mitchell does not have other plans,' cut in her mother. 'He and your father might have other business to discuss — more important issues.'

'Well actually, there is something . . . ' Jude began, only to be stopped mid-sentence.

'Let's eat first!' said Sir Joseph, as Dorothy served poached eggs and crispy bacon.

'And tonight,' Prudence continued, 'I shall play and sing for you again.'

He felt stifled. His plan was to leave after breakfast and find a room in the village.

'Jude, you do like my singing, don't you?'

Prudence spoke in that bleating tone again, needing the compliments as a thirsty man needed water.

'You have the voice of a nightingale,' he assured her, noting how she flashed an uncertain look at her mother to confirm it was a compliment. 'You are an absolute delight. The piece you played last night seemed particularly intricate. I admire your courage in tackling something so complex.'

Her face lit up. 'Yes, it is actually very difficult. It was written by a new young Hungarian composer named Frederic Chopin. That's right, isn't it, Mama?'

Hester seemed on the edge of intervening, to gloss over any chance remark by her daughter that might fail to impress him. She now acknowledged her daughter's musical prowess with a small smile and proud tilt of her chin. 'You've no need to ask me, Prudence. Music is your forte.'

Prudence blinked her pretty eyes. 'I often get mixed up with the composers, but Lily . . . ' She faltered, as if regretting bringing up Lily's name again unnecessarily; while the mere mention of her sent tremors through Jude's body. He inhaled deeply and somehow kept his composure as Prudence continued, 'Lily persuaded me to read a book about composers and musicians.'

'Good advice,' Jude agreed. 'Getting into the composer's mind will undoubtedly help you bring more passion into your playing.'

Hester put down her knife and fork. 'Prudence, after breakfast, why don't you show Mr Mitchell the book? He's very keen on reading and music.'

For a second, the look on Prudence's pretty face implied that she couldn't think of anything more boring than to look at a book. But when she realised her mother was offering an opportunity to be alone with him, her face lit up.

She glanced hopefully at him. 'Would you like to see it?'

Jude sighed inwardly. It was such an obvious ploy to push them together that for a moment he wasn't sure which of these women irritated him the most. But good manners prevailed. Besides, it might provide an opportunity of letting Prudence down gently.

'Yes, that would be most interesting,'

he said, continuing to eat his breakfast. He had the feeling it was going to be a long day.

After breakfast, he and Prudence strolled along to the library. Last night Lily had been in here. He hoped she would be again. His heart sank when he saw that she wasn't.

'Now then, where would it be?' Prudence mused, wandering around the book-lined room, looking totally out of place. 'It's here somewhere. It has a dark-blue cover.'

Before long, Prudence gave up looking and wandered back to him, a confident tilt to her head. Although she was a delight to the eyes, he pitied her for being so empty-headed. Yet she clearly had a brain to have mastered the piano so well, and to have learned how to read music. How sad that she didn't use that brain more often.

There was no point in delaying the moment any longer, but he needed to let her down gently. He took her hands in his. 'Prudence, you are a lovely young woman, and I'm sure that one day . . . ' He was about to say that the right man would come along and whisk her off her feet — but he wasn't that man.

But his initial compliment was enough to thrill her. She stretched up on tiptoes and kissed him.

The softness of her lips startled him. For a second he neither pulled away nor reciprocated. His intention was to nip all romantic thoughts on her part in the bud before she got hurt, not for her to kiss him. She stepped back, fluttering her eyelashes and smiling wickedly.

Something caught his eye — a movement in the doorway. Lily! He glimpsed her stunned expression before she turned and dashed away.

Prudence giggled. 'Goodness, I do hope Lily isn't shocked at seeing us kissing. Now, what were you going to say, Jude?'

He could have kicked himself. Why, oh why, had she walked in at that very moment? She would misconstrue this situation completely. And after all the declarations and promises of an hour earlier, it would brand him as a liar and a monster. He had to go to her, to try and put this right. But deep in his heart he feared the damage was already done.

* * *

The sight Lily had just witnessed had burned itself into her heart and soul. She ran from the house, holding back the tears, hurt beyond belief. After all he'd said to her, he'd been lying. It was all an act. Why hadn't she listened to her first instincts? From the very start she had sensed he was a womaniser, a philanderer. She was a complete and utter gullible fool.

She hated the man. Hated him!

Finding solitude in the orchard, Lily sank down onto the grass and gave way to scalding tears. What a liar he was.

Her heart broken she recalled how he had kissed her, held her. How he'd promised to put a ring on her finger.

She despised him, loathed him . . . loved him.

Then her tear-filled eyes widened, positive she could hear him calling her name. She moaned; she was becoming even more delusional.

She dried her eyes. The man wasn't worth shedding another tear over. She had little doubt, however, that he and Prudence would become betrothed and she would have to listen to Prudence regaling the most intimate details of their relationship.

Her head was throbbing. The thought of Jude making love to Prudence tore feverishly at her heart. She had to get away. She came to her decision quickly.

Today she would speak to Sir Joseph regarding her hopes of finding employment as an illustrator. Or, if he thought the idea too preposterous, then she would ask Lady Hester and Mrs Pritchard for references, and try to find work in service.

Doing her best to feel positive about the day ahead, Lily returned to the

201

house. She slipped quietly in, hoping not to disturb anyone. She knew that her eyes were puffy and red from crying, and her hair was a tangled mess. Before she spoke to anyone, she needed to wash her face and tidy herself up.

Alone in her upstairs room, Lily stripped out of her skirt and blouse. Standing in just a thin cotton petticoat, she poured water from the jug into a basin and washed. The sun was blazing in, and she pushed open the sash window to let in some fresh air and cool down. The fragrance from the rose garden drifted up, filling her room with its scent.

She knelt on her bed, gazing far across the garden and the countryside that had so long been her home. It was a magnificent view with distant woodlands and fields of green and yellow. She would miss this. But she couldn't stay with Jude and Prudence becoming betrothed or lovers. She just couldn't.

A movement just beneath her window caught her eye, and she

glanced down. Jude was standing on the paving blatantly staring up at her. And then she realised why. She was wearing just the flimsy petticoat, and the warm breeze had moulded the fabric to her breasts. With a gasp, she drew back from the window, her cheeks flaming.

Her embarrassment turned to anger. It was downright discourteous that he hadn't looked away on seeing she wasn't properly dressed, instead of standing there gawking.

Minutes later, a tap on her bedroom door made her jump. It would be Prudence.

'Just a moment,' she called, snatching up her clothing and bracing herself to listen to Prudence's latest exploits with Jude Mitchell. She really did not want to hear about them kissing.

But it wasn't Prudence whose head peered around the door. It was Jude. In one deft movement he was in her room and the door closed behind him.

'How dare you!' Lily exclaimed,

clutching her blouse to her breasts. 'Get out!'

'Lily, I need to speak to you, to explain.'

She couldn't bear to look at him. 'Would you please get out of my room!'

He spoke in a whisper. 'Lily, what you saw . . . '

'I saw you kissing Prudence. After all you'd said to me. What a fool I am.' She amazed herself with her control of her voice, but her eyes blazed. 'Now get out of my room!'

But he took a step towards her. '*She* kissed *me* . . . '

'Oh, so that makes a difference, does it?'

He dragged his fingers raggedly through his hair. 'I know I've totally given you the wrong impression of me . . . '

'No. You've given me the *right* impression. I thought you were a womaniser from the moment I set eyes on you. And now I *know* you're a cheat and a cad! I pity Prudence . . . '

'Prudence has nothing to do with this. I'll be out of her life by the end of the day.' He closed the space between them. 'But I want you *in* my life. Lily Baines, I *need* you in my life.'

Despite her anger and outrage, there was something in his eyes that made Lily doubt what she had seen. Could she have interpreted the situation wrongly? A tremulous feeling stirred in her breast, as if the tiniest seed of hope had sprung back into life.

The sudden opening of her bedroom door startled them both. Prudence stood there, her excited expression turning instantly to surprise — and then her chin crumpled and her eyes welled up with tears. Her pouting mouth opened and she wailed, 'Mama!'

Angrily, Lily pushed past Jude to reach her dear friend. 'Oh Prudence, now do you see why I was trying to warn you? He's not to be trusted. He's a womaniser.'

Prudence threw Lily's hands off her. 'Don't touch me! Don't speak to me!'

She backed away, her hands clenched into fists. 'You've been jealous of me and Jude from the very start. Now you've tricked him into your bedroom. How could you?'

Lily gasped. 'I've done no such thing! Prudence, listen to me.'

'And you've hardly any clothes on!' Without warning, Prudence slapped Lily across the cheek.

Lily recoiled, more from astonishment than because it hurt. In a flash Jude stepped between them. He firmly eased Prudence out of the room.

'This is not Lily's doing,' he stated. 'I needed to speak to her. I barged in uninvited which was very wrong. But this is none of her doing. She's been telling me to go from the very second I set foot — '

'Well it didn't look like that to me!' Prudence said, pouting all the more, but not throwing Jude's hands off her.

Lady Hester came running up the stairs. 'What's going on? What are you all doing?'

'Madam, I apologise,' said Jude, looking wretchedly at Lily, the most earnest pleading look in his eyes. Then his head dropped. 'I'll get my things and leave.'

'You'll do no such thing,' dismissed Lady Hester. 'I would appreciate you leaving us to talk for a few minutes. I trust you will be courteous enough to remain here until I have got to the bottom of this matter.' She glared as angrily at her daughter as at Lily. 'Make yourself decent, Lily, and come downstairs at once. Prudence, come!'

If it hadn't been for one cheek burning red from where Prudence had slapped her, there would have been no colour in Lily's face at all. She felt sick to the very soul. The family who had been so good to her were furious. She had betrayed them all.

The two women were waiting for her on the landing, as if she couldn't be trusted not to follow Jude into *his* bedroom. Hester indicated that she lead the way downstairs. They followed her like a pair of jailers guarding their prisoner.

'Into my study,' snapped Lady Hester.

Lily went in, wondering whether Sir Joseph was aware of all the commotion.

Lady Hester's tone was clipped, her expression sour and pinched. 'What happened?'

'Jude was in her bedroom, Mama, and she'd hardly any clothes on.'

Every part of Hester's face screwed up tight, as if she were sucking a lemon. 'You slept with him?'

'No! Of course I didn't,' Lily said, totally outraged. 'He knocked at my door just a minute ago and barged in. I told him to get out, but he wouldn't.'

Prudence began tugging at the corners of her lace handkerchief. 'I don't believe her, Mama.'

'Neither do I,' uttered Lady Hester, her dull grey-blue eyes narrowing to slits. 'There's been something going on from the very start. You're a jealous little vixen, Lily Baines, wanting some-one else's man. Just like your mother!'

Lily saw something in Hester's eyes then, a flash of hatred. It could only mean one thing, and yet Lily couldn't comprehend that. There was no time to think. Hester's next words left her stunned.

'You'll leave today. Right now! This very minute. Pack your belongings.'

Lily felt her legs buckle beneath her. Prudence looked uncertain for a moment, and then she tilted her chin smugly.

'But where shall I go?' Lily managed to utter.

'I really don't care.'

Prudence gave a nervous kind of giggle. 'She has to go somewhere, Mama. She can't just sleep in a ditch.'

'More's the pity,' said Lady Hester, levelling her gaze at Lily. 'You see how kind this family is to you? You try and break up my daughter's relationship and the dear girl is still concerned for you.'

Lily couldn't speak. Desperately she wanted to defend herself; only, deep down, she was as guilty as they said she was.

Lady Hester paced across the room, leaving Prudence and Lily watching her as she decided what to do. Then she spun round and glared at Lily. 'For today, at least, you'll go and work with Ted Draper. His account books need to be brought up to date. Once he's set you to work, send him to see me. But you'll stay there until you hear from me. Do you understand?'

Lily nodded, relieved not to have been thrown out the door. She would make this up to Prudence, and to the rest of the family, even though it hadn't really been her doing. It was that wretched Jude Mitchell who had caused all this upset. She truly hated the man.

Finally dismissed by a stern-faced Hester and equally sullen Prudence, Lily ran back to her room and dressed. It took all her willpower not to barge into Jude's bedroom and tell him exactly what she thought of him.

Somehow she resisted the urge. Instead, she dressed and had breakfast, explaining to Mrs Pritchard that she would be at Ted Draper's farm today. She said nothing about Jude barging into her room and landing her in trouble with the family. That was just too embarrassing.

Lily half-expected to bump into Jude as she set out towards the farm. But he was nowhere to be seen. Hanging his head in shame, Lily hoped. Yet, as she walked briskly along the narrow lane, the realisation dawned that Jude might well have left by the time she returned home, and she would most likely never set eyes on him again. The thought made her heart feel as heavy as a lump of clay.

Ted Draper was delighted to have her company for the day, as were his four children. And while Lily worked on the account ledgers, Ted's eldest child, Hannah, kept her well-fed with buttered scones and sweet damson jam, and the little ones played around her feet and in the yard.

Lily was glad of being so occupied, as thoughts of Jude Mitchell were pushed to the darker recesses of her mind, which was a blessed relief.

There was a dull ache over Lily's eyes when she finally placed the pencil down on the table and closed the ledgers with a relieved sigh. Her work had taken her until late afternoon to finish, and her back ached with sitting still for so long.

'Ah! Here's Father!' Hannah exclaimed as the back door opened.

The younger children ran to greet him, and Ted Draper swept them up in his arms.

'Your accounts are all finished, Ted,' said Lily. 'I'll be getting back now . . . '

Ted set his children down, a strange sadness clouding his eyes. 'Thank you, Lily. I'm most grateful. Children, come and give Lily a hug. She's going now. Then, Hannah, get the little ones some milk.'

Lily went around the room, getting a

hug from each child. 'I'll see you all soon — and thank you for my meals, Hannah. You're a wonderful cook!'

The girl looked pleased. She was coping well as the lady of the house. In a way, she was an inspiration to Lily. If a child could take care of a household, then she could too. She would make plans to find a proper job as soon as possible.

Ted opened the latched door and she followed him across the cobbled yard to the open gateway that led to the lane. But as she went to bid him good afternoon, he put a hand on her forearm. His face was wreathed in sadness as he said, 'You can't go home, Lily.'

She stared at him, not understanding for a second. 'Oh! Of course. Did Lady Hester say when . . . '

'Lily, I don't know what's gone on, and I don't want to know,' said Ted, not looking at her but gazing off down the lane. 'But something's made her blazing mad. She's . . . she's . . . '

'She's what, Ted?' Lily asked, frowning so hard her head ached.

'She's sending a carriage for you.'

'But I don't need a carriage, I can walk back . . . ' As she spoke she saw a horse-drawn carriage heading this way.

Ted took her hand between his, and squeezed. There were tears in his eyes.

'Ted?'

He cleared his throat as the carriage rattled to a stop. 'She told me to tell you you're moving to London.' He fumbled in his pocket for a large envelope. 'The driver's got the address. And here's a letter of introduction to the lady you're to be working for. And there's some money in here too.'

Lily rocked on her heels. 'You mean, I'm to leave — now? Not return home at all to say goodbye — to get my clothes, my books?'

She followed his gaze and saw the large trunk battened down on the roof of the carriage. 'My things?' she gasped.

He nodded.

Her knees buckled and Ted caught

her. 'I can't just leave ... I can't. Please, Ted, let me go and speak to her ...'

'Lily, she's given me my orders. I'm so sorry.'

The carriage driver, a dour, long-faced man, looked down from his seat. 'I ain't got all day.'

Ted pressed the envelope into her hands then stepped back. Lily's world swam. A swirling black void took the place of rational thought, and as if in a dream she stepped up to the carriage door and turned the handle. It swung open. For one second she prayed that Jude Mitchell had been sent packing too. But the carriage was as empty and desolate as her heart.

She climbed aboard. Ted closed the door after her, and the carriage gave a jolt as it set off. Lily fell back against the leather seats, too distraught to cry. At least for the first hour. Then she sobbed quietly until they had reached the smog and slums of London town.

11

Jude spent the most frustrating day ever. After the early-morning fiasco, the women of the house went strangely silent. Sir Joseph, who seemed completely in the dark about the situation, insisted on showing him more of the estate.

Jude was desperate to see Lily. Prudence had been quick in slapping her; he prayed that Hester hadn't taken further action. But there was neither sight nor sound of either woman.

'Sir,' began Jude, as he and Sir Joseph came away from a dairy farm with a fine cheese for the manor's larder. 'You may not have heard, but I've fallen out of favour with your good wife and daughter. I acted rather foolishly this morning . . . '

Sir Joseph put a hand on his arm. 'We all act foolishly where beautiful women are concerned. I'm sure no harm was done.'

'Sadly, a great deal of harm was done . . . '

'Your intentions, Jude,' Sir Joseph interrupted him. 'Are we to make plans for a wedding between my daughter and your good self? I know Prudence is enamoured with you. Are those feelings reciprocated?'

Jude heaved a sigh. 'I wish I could say so; but unfortunately, beautiful and enchanting though she is, we are not compatible. I'm sure she would tire of me in no time.'

It was the older man's turn to sigh. 'Ah! I thought as much. I appreciate your words. Say no more, Jude. I understand.'

'I can't take advantage of your hospitality any longer, sir,' added Jude. 'I need to arrange for a carriage at the earliest opportunity, and be on my way.'

'I'm sorry to see you go. But stay for dinner tonight, and we'll get you on tomorrow's carriage.'

It was a relief to know he had another chance of speaking to Lily. And as they continued their tour he made plans. He'd write a letter and slip it under her door. He would provide his address, so that if she wanted, she could contact him. That was a last resort. What he needed to do was to somehow try and make her understand how deeply he cared about her.

Eventually the day came to an end. 'I don't know about you, Jude, but I'm more than ready for my dinner,' said Sir Joseph.

'Indeed I am,' Jude agreed, although food was the last thing on his mind.

He wasn't looking forward to seeing Hester and Prudence; but to his surprise, neither seemed to be harbouring a grudge against him. Prudence had clearly gone to a great deal of effort to display her ample charms for his delight again. She wasn't the sullen young lady he'd expected. There was a sparkle in her eye while Hester was the picture of graciousness as dinner was served.

Jude had no appetite. He needed Lily but there was no sign of her.

Sir Joseph made an effort in keeping the conversation flowing, thankfully not mentioning that this was their final meal together. No mention either of betrothals — or, rather, the lack of one. As the evening wore on, Jude waited for an opportunity of thanking them all for their hospitality and wishing Prudence a happy life.

She had been unusually quiet throughout the meal, although she had glanced constantly to her mother as if waiting for her to say something. The feeling that there was something he didn't know about was starting to play heavily on his mind.

They had almost finished eating when the news came.

Lady Hester placed her knife and fork neatly on her plate and looked at her husband. 'Joseph, dear, we had quite a surprise today.'

He smiled at her. 'Did you, my love?'

'Yes. Lily upped and left.'

Sir Joseph almost choked. A deep redness swept up his neck into his face. And the word came out as a gasp. 'Left?'

Jude felt his world drop away.

'Yes, just announced to Prudence and I that she had secured some position as a housekeeper.'

'What does Lily know about housekeeping?' Sir Joseph blurted out, gripping the edges of the table now, as if he might fall off his chair.

'Well, exactly,' Hester said as if agreeing. 'That's what I said. But I understand that the cook has been giving her tuition on housekeeping. I checked, and it's true. Not that Mrs Pritchard knew what she had planned.'

'But to just leave, without a word . . . ' uttered Sir Joseph. 'Where has she gone? Who is she working for? Do we know them? Is it someone local?'

Jude sat silently, a pain in his heart that equalled his pain of losing Isabella. Sir Joseph looked distraught, but he was asking all the right questions.

Lady Hester remained totally unemotional. 'You know as much as me, dear. Lily simply made her announcement, picked up her bags and left. She'd already packed her things and had arranged a carriage. Prudence and I were in shock, weren't we, Prudence?'

'Dreadfully shocked,' Prudence agreed, but her expression said otherwise. She was loving this and Jude had no doubt that Hester was too. There was a certain glee in her words and the offhand way she was treating this.

He felt sick to the very soul. He guessed Lily hadn't just 'upped and left' of her own accord. This was all down to him being found in her room this morning. They'd sent her packing. Probably thinking that with Lily out of the way, it left the passage clear for him and Prudence.

What an idiot he was. His selfishness of wanting her had lost Lily her home. And she had no family. She had told him that. He had destroyed Lily's life.

Dear God, they came no worse than him.

His thoughts were rocked suddenly when, to everyone's astonishment, Sir Joseph leapt to his feet, sending his chair flying across the room. He thumped his fists so hard on the table that plates clattered and two glasses toppled over and shattered, wine spilled across the linen tablecloth.

Gleeful expressions on Prudence and Hester's faces were exchanged for alarm.

'I *don't* know as much as you!' Sir Joseph raged at his wife. 'You were here. I wasn't! Why didn't you stop her, at least until I came home?'

Jude placed a hand on the man's arm, finding that he was trembling.

Hester was trembling too, with anger. 'I don't care to be spoken to in that tone, Joseph, particularly in front of our guest.'

Sir Joseph ran a hand through his thinning hair. 'I apologise . . . to you all. It's just such a — a shock. Hester, please think carefully. Did Lily give you any clue as to where she was going?'

The woman sat stiffly, her chin tilted angrily. 'She said something about London, and that she would write once she was settled in.'

'London?' Sir Joseph breathed, his head going down, a broken man.

Jude was suddenly aware of the situation. There was no doubt about it. No wonder he'd thought Lily was Sir Joseph's daughter when he first set eyes on her. No wonder Lady Hester was so hostile towards her. Yet Lily hadn't known — hadn't seen it with her own eyes.

It was so obvious. And if there was ever any doubt that Sir Joseph was Lily's father, it was evident by his concern and anguish now that he was.

He understood, too, the flippant manner in which Lady Hester had given him the news, as if daring her husband to make a fuss and admit it was his daughter who had walked out of his life, not just a servant girl.

Jude picked up the chair that had toppled over and placed it beneath the older man. Gently, he pressed him down into his seat and poured him a brandy. He took over the line of questioning, positive that these two women knew more than they were saying.

'Prudence, I'm sure you had a dozen questions to ask Lily. You don't look the sort of young lady to allow a friend to begin an adventure in London without telling you all her plans.' He looked candidly at her. 'You *are* her friend, aren't you?'

'Well, of course. We're almost like . . . ' She stopped in mid-sentence and changed tack. 'Of course I asked, but Lily can be secretive sometimes, can't she, Mama?'

'Very secretive,' Hester agreed, her back rigid and shoulders set defiantly.

'So, no hint of where she's gone?' continued Jude, not believing a word of this. Clearly they had taken the opportunity of Sir Joseph being out of the house to dismiss her. Get rid of his illegitimate daughter once and for all. And it was all Jude's fault.

'As I said, London,' stated Hester, all but turning her head aside.

'And the carriage — did you know the driver?' Jude continued, wanting to shake her.

'I didn't look. When Lily closed that front door behind her, washing her hands of us after all we've done for her, I was too hurt to chase after her.'

Sir Joseph sat with his head in his hands. 'I don't understand. Wouldn't she have needed a reference to get a job? Am I such an ogre that she hasn't even mentioned her thoughts to me?'

Despite his own misery, Jude's heart went out to Lily's father. He put a hand on the man's shoulder. 'Would you excuse me?' He strode from the room, not waiting for an answer, and bounded up the stairs to the top floor.

Pushing open Lily's bedroom door, his heart lurched. It was stripped bare. The bed and the tallboy remained, but nothing else. No books, no paints or paintings, no knick-knacks, no clothing. All of which he'd noticed that morning.

And no note for him.

Lily had indeed gone.

He went to his own room before going back downstairs, just in case Lily had slipped a note under his door. The despair was almost too much when he saw that she had not.

Hoping the staff would be more forthcoming, Jude went through to the kitchen. The cook and the young maid were sitting with cups of tea, looking quite forlorn.

'Please don't get up,' Jude said, wondering how much they knew. How much they had witnessed this afternoon. The looks on their faces indicated their dismay that Lily had left so suddenly.

'Ladies, I need to know — the family needs to know. Do you know where Lily has gone? Did she give you a forwarding address?

The cook's eyes were red-rimmed. 'I

don't know, sir.'

'Then what do you know? How was Lily when she left? Was she upset?'

'We didn't see her. Last I seen of her was when she was setting off to do Ted Draper's accounts at his farm this morning. There was some commotion this afternoon. Two chaps from the estate came and loaded a trunk onto a carriage. I'd no idea it was Lily's things, not till her ladyship came and gave us the news that Lily wouldn't be back.'

'I reckon they gave her her marching orders!' Dorothy exclaimed. 'I saw Lady Hester and Miss Prudence in Lily's room earlier. They must have been packing her stuff.'

'Now don't you be making wild assumptions, young lady,' the cook chided. 'If they say Lily's got work in service, then that's what happened.'

The expressions on both the cook's and Dorothy's faces told him they were as saddened and shocked as Sir Joseph was. He put his hand on the cook's shoulder. 'You've known Lily a long time?'

The woman sniffed; then, making out she'd got a cold, she blew her nose. 'Her mam was my scullery maid. I've known Lily since she was a baby. I can't believe she'd just up and leave us without a word.'

'It weren't her doing . . . ' Dorothy practically shouted.

'Hush!' the cook warned again. 'Take heed. If you value your job and a good roof over your head, you'll keep your thoughts to yourself.'

Jude spoke kindly. 'I'm sure Lily would not have left so abruptly if she'd had the choice. And I'm sure she'll be in touch when she can.'

Back in his room, Jude packed, moving automatically, too distraught to think ahead. This whole episode had been disastrous. Totally disastrous — and the blame was his. He deserved the pain in his heart at losing Lily. The others — Sir Joseph, the cook, and the maid — didn't deserve to have their hearts broken.

He took his trunk downstairs and left it in the hall. He found Sir Joseph alone in the library.

The man looked soulfully up as Jude entered. 'I thought I'd find a letter here, on my desk. A note to tell me she was going. I can't believe she's gone . . . I can't bear it . . . ' He put his head down onto the desk and wept.

Jude stood close and rested his hand on the man's shaking shoulder. After a moment, he asked quietly, 'You never told Lily, did you?'

Sir Joseph stilled for a moment as the question sunk in, and then with a huge sigh he shook his head. Jude remained where he was, patting his shoulder as if it were some comfort.

Eventually Sir Joseph blew his nose and mopped his eyes. 'I'm sorry. It's not the done thing for a man to cry.'

'Some things are worth crying over,' Jude murmured. 'Was her mother very much like Lily?'

Sir Joseph's eyes fluttered shut, as if

the pain were unbearable. And then he nodded. 'Lily is almost the double of her mother. My wife could see that too, and I think that's why she didn't stop Lily from leaving today. And who can blame her?'

'Yes, I think that could be the case,' Jude agreed, not voicing his thoughts that Lily had had no choice in going. 'Lily told me that her mother had died in childbirth.'

'Lillian was a maid here. And I fell in love with her.' He glanced at Jude, shame in his eyes. 'Of course it was wrong. I was married, my wife was expecting Prudence . . . but I'd fallen hopelessly in love with her.'

'We cannot help who we fall in love with,' said Jude with a heavy heart.

Sir Joseph breathed deeply. 'Lillian told no one she was pregnant, not even me. Somehow she hid it beneath loose clothing. She was slim — frail, really. I can see that now, looking back.' A small wistful smile appeared on his face. 'Lily has grown up so like her mother, yet sturdier, much stronger and healthier, thankfully.'

The older man got to his feet and poured himself a small brandy, offering a glass to Jude, who shook his head. Taking a sip of his drink, he continued, 'The first anyone knew of Lillian's pregnancy was when she went into labour. We were all in shock — Mrs Pritchard, Hester, me. By the time we'd sent for a midwife, the baby was here. Mrs Pritchard and I delivered her. Hester just stood in the corner of the kitchen glaring at me. She saw then that I was the father. I couldn't hide my feelings — my utter joy when a little baby girl was born . . . ' He finished his drink in one gulp. 'And my despair when Lillian passed away in my arms a few hours later.'

Jude lowered Sir Joseph onto the sofa, and sat beside him as he sobbed.

When his emotions were again under control, Sir Joseph continued, 'I've watched Lily grow and become the lovely young woman that she is. Time after time I've wanted to tell her the truth.' He looked at Jude. 'But guilt for hurting my wife kept me from telling Lily I was her father. You know, Hester has never spoken of it, never said that she knew.'

Jude nodded his head. 'Does Prudence know?'

He shook his head. 'I should have told her, and I think at times it has crossed her mind. She needs to know she has a sister — well, a half-sister. I will tell her, soon.'

'Yes, I think you should. And you should tell Lily.' He didn't voice his fears that Sir Joseph might already have missed his chance. He'd possibly never see her again.

'I almost told her on her birthday — almost. Then, like the coward I am, I didn't.' He looked desperately at Jude. 'Find her for me, Jude. Please, please help me find her.'

'Of course.' He didn't need to be asked. He had to find Lily to beg forgiveness for wrecking her life, and to prove that he loved her.

Jude left before breakfast. On impulse, he discreetly left his card with the cook, and a request that she contact him if she learned of Lily's whereabouts.

Prudence remained in her room as he said his goodbyes to Sir Joseph and his wife. Lady Hester returned indoors as Sir Joseph walked with him to his carriage.

'I'm sorry your visit has not been as successful as we'd hoped,' said Sir Joseph, the sadness still there in his eyes.

'I am deeply sorry too, sir.'

The older man clutched Jude's arm as he stepped up into the carriage. 'Jude, please, find Lily. Bring her home.'

'I will,' he promised, though God alone knew how he would in a city the size of London.

There were tears in the older man's eyes as he stepped away from the carriage.

As the vehicle clattered away, Jude looked back at the house, half-imagining he could see Lily gathering windfalls in the orchard, her golden hair flying wildly in the breeze. And then he imagined her in his arms, tilting her lovely face up to his, kissing him.

The long, arduous journey back to London was the most painful Jude had ever endured.

12

The journey into London passed in an endless hazy blur. Lily's head throbbed. Her life had been turned upside down — and all because of Jude Mitchell. With every passing mile, she felt more alone, more afraid, and more angry with the man.

As the carriage rattled on, narrow country lanes opened up on to wider roads. They crossed an iron structured bridge that spanned a river. She guessed it was the River Thames. Under different circumstances it would have been exciting to see the capital city of England. She'd read so much about London in Sir Joseph's library that she knew she'd be able to pick out the famous landmarks quite easily. But her heart was too heavy to take an interest.

The thought of never seeing Sir

Joseph again sent another wave of sadness flooding over her. Did he know of her departure? And what of Mrs Pritchard? Not being able to say goodbye to them was heartbreaking. And what would they think of her?

Lady Hester would have made up some story regarding her departure. She dreaded to think what that might have been.

As for Jude Mitchell, she hoped he was ashamed of himself. Did he know that she had lost her home? She doubted he would even care.

Travelling on, Lily noted a marked change in the noise of the carriage wheels and the horses' hooves. There was sharpness now, a clatter as lanes became cobbled streets and the air became thick with the smell of smoke and grime. The views of open country-side closed in, and Lily found herself hemmed in by huge imposing buildings of grey stone, then narrow grimy streets. She shuddered at the dull drabness of London. It stank of smog and filth; there was no freshness, no sweet smell of hay or flowers. How could anyone bear to live here?

Raggedy children were playing in the streets, many without shoes and in tattered pinafores and breeches, with dirty hands and dirty faces. There were drunken men and ugly women. She caught snatches of conversation as the carriage passed by. The language was foul and harsh. She wanted to pull down the blind and shut it all out, but the next moment, the carriage lurched to a standstill.

'We're here, miss.'

'We can't be,' Lily murmured, staring out at a row of dull terraced houses, black rails with steps leading up to front doors with paint peeling off, and basements with windows caked in grime. Her heart felt like lead. All the way here, she had clung to the hope that the person she would be working for would be decent and kind. She couldn't imagine Lady Hester being acquainted with anyone who lived in such a place as this. Although the houses were towering four-storied affairs, and might at one time have looked grand, to her they appeared miserable and neglected.

The carriage driver opened the door for her, much to the amusement of a group of men and women hanging about on the steps of the house. The men whistled, and Lily heard the mocking 'La de da!' comment from a woman who, Lily noticed, wore a dress even more revealing than anything Prudence had in her wardrobe.

There was nothing attractive about these women, though. They looked indecently provocative, and Lily saw the carriage driver's eyes widen as he risked a swift glance at them.

'This can't be the right address,' Lily said, not wanted to get out.

'I'm afraid it is. I'll get your trunk down and be on me way.'

'No! You've made a mistake . . . '

'I've been paid to drop you off here, miss.' He gave her a slip of paper with the address written in Lady Hester's hand.

He was eager to be on his way. The men hanging about looked rough, and were watching with growing interest. No doubt her driver was afraid of being robbed.

He deposited her trunk on the pavement. 'Weighs a ruddy ton. Want me to drag it up the steps?'

Lily's heart was sinking. She really was going to be abandoned here, in this wretched place with these frightening strangers. Panic welled up inside her.

The driver spoke impatiently. 'I ain't got all day. Up the steps or not?'

'Up the steps, please,' she answered flatly.

The bystanders were eyeing her up and down. The younger woman gave her a small sympathetic smile. 'You moving in, love?'

'Yes, I . . . I think so. I'm looking for . . . ' She checked the letter Hester had given her. 'A Mrs Caldwell. Are you . . . ?'

The older woman laughed, a harsh laugh. Her teeth were stained brown and she had a bruise around her eye.

'I'll be off then, miss. There's nothing to pay,' interrupted the driver. 'The mistress at the manor paid me in advance. Good luck.' Under his breath, he murmured, 'You're going to need it.'

The group mimicked *the manor*, mincing about, pretending to put on airs and graces.

Lily ignored them, feeling numb as the driver climbed back into position and urged the horses to move on.

'Well, he couldn't get his backside out of here any quicker, could he?'

Lily turned to the girl who had spoken. She looked about her own age, but there was a sunken hollowness to her cheeks and shadows beneath her eyes. She had some sort of rouge on her cheekbones and her hair was piled on top of her head in an untidy bundle.

'I'm looking for Mrs Caldwell, she lives here. Do you know her? I've a letter of introduction . . . '

The girl's hand curled around Lily's forearm; there was a rim of black beneath each fingernail. She spoke kindly. 'She's dead, love.'

Lily stared at her. 'What? What did you say?'

'Popped her clogs, me duck. A long time ago. This place is rented out now, and packed to the hilt.'

Lily felt a wave of dizziness wash over her. 'No, that can't be right . . . '

'It's right enough. Dead before I moved here. Aggie knew her, though; didn't you, Aggie?'

The older woman was in an embrace with one of the men. His hands were all over her. Lily gasped and turned away, glad of the railings to cling on to. In her mind's eye she could suddenly see herself living on the streets, in a shop doorway. The dizziness became a swamping feeling, making it difficult to breathe.

The girl's hand on her arm tightened. 'So what's your name, then?'

'Lily, Lily Baines,' she uttered, trying

to focus, trying to think straight, trying not to give way to panic.

'You been chucked out? Been messing about, and your old man kicked you out?'

'Old man?' Lily murmured.

'Yeah, your husband. Must want his head looking at, chucking you out. You're really pretty.'

'I'm not married, but yes, I have been thrown out of my home.'

'Catch you stealing, did they? That's what happened to me.'

'No! I've never stolen a thing in my life!' Lily answered, so annoyed at the suggestion that she felt some fire returning to her soul.

The girl backed off, grinning a cheeky smile. 'I believe you. You don't look the type to go nicking stuff. So that's all right, then. I'll trust you. Come on!'

The front door with its peeling paintwork was open, and the girl gave it a push with her foot. She grabbed the handle of Lily's trunk at the same time.

'What are you doing?'

'You can share with me.' She pulled a face. 'Well, give me a hand, then; this thing weighs a ton. What you got in it, the kitchen sink?'

'I've no idea,' Lily murmured, not knowing if Hester had packed all her things, her books and art materials, or not.

The house smelled of damp and mildew. There was a red-tiled corridor and wide staircase: clearly it had once been a grand home — no doubt in the days of Hester's acquaintance, Mrs Caldwell. But now it was dirty and battered and ugly.

Someone was arguing upstairs. A stream of curses and swear words rang out before a man came stumbling down the stairs at a pace that implied someone had given him a hearty push. A woman, screaming abuse, appeared on the landing wearing nothing but a thin nightgown. She flung a pair of boots down after him. Lily dodged aside as the man and the boots came clattering downstairs.

Seeing Lily, he stopped in his tracks and gave her a leering smile. 'Now, you'd be worth paying a couple of bob for.'

The young woman at Lily's side jerked her thumb, indicating he should clear off. 'She's out of your league, matey. Go on, sling yer hook.'

Lily watched him hopping about getting his boots on as he departed. 'Does he live here?'

'No, love, he just visits now and then.' She cocked her head to one side. 'You in trouble? Y'know, up the duff?'

'What?' It dawned on her then what she meant. 'Heavens, no . . . '

The other woman shrugged and went into one of the rooms, dragging Lily's trunk after her. 'Home sweet home. Come on in. Oh, and I'm Tilda, short for Matilda.'

Lily followed her, grateful to have a roof over her head. The room was slightly bigger than her bedroom at the manor and seemed fairly clean. There was a single bed on one side of the room, and a mattress on the floor on the other. In between was a wardrobe with a cracked mirror, some shelves, and a hearth with a kettle and iron pot standing on a grid.

'Hope you've got your own bedsheets cos I ain't got any spare,' said Tilda, dragging the trunk across the wooden floorboards closer to the mattress.

'You're very kind, Tilda,' Lily murmured. 'You don't know me, and yet you've just taken me in off the streets.'

Tilda shrugged and flashed a cheeky smile. 'It's me good turn for the day. Maybe God in His heaven will clock this up and forget all the wicked things I've done when I get up there.'

'I'm sure He will,' Lily said, and for the first time that day, attempted a small smile — it failed miserably.

13

Jude stood at the fourth-floor warehouse window looking down at the quayside of St Katharine's Docks. T. J. Mitchell & Son was one of the many merchant businesses trading here. Steamships were moored at the quayside, and sailing ships with their canvas sails rolled up lay anchored out in the estuary. The docks were bustling with activity and commotion as cargo was loaded and unloaded. Men were busy climbing rigging or hoisting crates and barrels in and out of ships' holds.

From up here the noises were muffled, but down on the docks it would be rife with banter and arguments, horses and carts transporting goods to grocers and distributors. These were exciting times for traders. Teas, coffees, cocoa, spices and tobacco were all in great demand. And, foolishly, he had dared to dream of sharing this life with Lily Baines.

He prayed she was all right. Wherever she was, he hoped she was being treated well. He was no nearer to finding her despite placing an advertisement in the paper asking for anyone knowing her whereabouts to contact him. Every day he'd walked the streets in the better-off areas of the city where they might need the services of a maid. He'd knocked on doors and had in desperation even shouted out her name. In return he'd received strange glances from passers-by, and no hint of where she might be.

From the window, the Thames Estuary looked a dark charcoal grey. It matched his black mood. He was back to where he was, feeling as low and wretched as when Isabella had passed — worse, even. What insanity had made him claw his way out of those depths of despair only to plunge straight back into them?

Someone knocked on his glass-panelled door and entered. 'Mr Mitchell, sir.'

Jude's hopes rose for a second. He'd given his foreman, Arthur Bateman, the task of checking daily with the newspaper. 'Any news, Arthur?'

'No news as such, sir, just a stock check of supplies and the passenger list. I can log it if you're busy . . . '

The spark of hope died, but Jude saw the worried look on his foreman's face. Arthur Bateman had worked for the company some twenty years. No doubt his employer in such a melancholy mood was something he hadn't seen since Isabella's death.

'Mr Mitchell?' Arthur enquired. 'Are you all right, sir?'

Jude was far from all right, but that would have to change. He had a business to run. The lives of dozens of families depended on him. Determinedly, he pulled himself together and strode towards the office door. 'I will be, Arthur, I will be. And I'm sorry if

I've left you holding the reins recently.'

'It's no trouble, sir. I'm just concerned. It's not like you . . . '

'You're quite right. It's not like me,' Jude said, taking the paperwork from him. 'There's work to be done, and we want the *Jenny Lyn* ready to set sail by the end of the week.'

'Aye, sir. We've plenty of orders for Persian rugs and ceramics since our last trip. And steerage is up to capacity.'

'*Our* capacity, I trust?' Jude enquired, knowing the *Jenny Lyn* could take twice as many paying passengers in theory, but preferring to take fewer and give everyone better conditions under which to travel.

'Naturally, sir.'

'Good man.' Jude hoped he sounded more himself. Sailing down through the Straits of Gibraltar needed a captain with all his wits about him, not a ship governed by some lovelorn dreamer.

It would be a month-long voyage. Would there be news of Lily when he got back? Doubts crowded him. Perhaps he should stay and keep searching. Arthur could handle the *Jenny Lyn*; he'd captained many a ship.

The anxious look on his foreman's face tipped the balance. He strode from the office and down the flights of stone steps to the quayside, Arthur at his heels. His ship and his crew awaited.

Somehow he had to push all thoughts of Lily Baines out of his head.

★ ★ ★

The soles of Lily's feet were on fire. London's cobbled streets were hot and rough. Every day for the past week she had walked miles, knocking on doors, asking for work, assuring strangers that she was a good, hardworking woman and entirely trustworthy. It would have helped to have letters of reference. Mrs Pritchard would surely have given her a reference given the opportunity. One or two house owners had noted her name and address in case a position become vacant. Lily clung to the hope that something would materialise.

It was almost dark as Lily returned to the house she now called home. Tilda and Aggie were standing on the steps trying to catch the eye of any passing man. It wasn't difficult. Lily herself had been stopped on numerous occasions and asked the price for her favours.

Tonight was no different. A rather shy young man approached her. Calmly, she directed him towards the two women. 'I'm not for sale,' Lily said pleasantly. 'Tilda — over there with the mop of hair — is nice, though. You should speak to her.'

The man actually blushed as he dragged the cap from his head and clutched it to his chest. 'I beg your pardon, I thought . . . '

'I know what you thought, but you are mistaken.'

He looked ready to curl up and die of shame. 'I don't normally do this kind of thing . . . '

'You don't need to explain to me. It's

those ladies you want.'

He looked at the three women, laughing so loudly that Lily quite understood his terror at approaching them. They could eat him alive. Wringing his cap like it was a dishcloth, he backed away. 'I'll be off, I reckon. Sorry I mistook you for, for . . . '

'It doesn't matter, really,' Lily assured him, and almost laughed as he turned and fled.

Tilda strolled up the street to meet her. 'Hello, Lily love; any luck?'

She shook her head. 'Not really, although there was a nice woman in Bayswater who wrote my name and address down really carefully, even double-checked it, as if she might get in touch. Fingers crossed!'

Tilda linked her arm. 'They want their 'eads looking at, the lot of 'em.'

As usual in the evenings, there was a pot of stew on the hob in the kitchen. Everyone used the communal kitchen and Ruthie, the oldest woman in the house, took it on herself to ensure there was always a hot meal and bread. Everyone chipped in with sixpence a week to buy the vegetables and scrag end of lamb or whatever else she could get hold of, so thankfully no one went very hungry.

Lily spooned out two bowlfuls and cut two chunks of bread. She and Tilda went back to their room to eat. It was something of a routine now, unless Tilda was entertaining a man. Then Lily ate in the kitchen. It reminded her of home, except that Mrs Pritchard would have a fit if she saw the state of this kitchen.

Occasionally, Lily had taken a break from job-hunting, and sat sketching some of the street people. She'd even sketched Tilda and tacked the picture above her bed.

Tonight, Lily was glad to lie down. Her feet were blistered and her limbs ached from walking. She fell asleep almost at once, but awoke in the night to hear the unmistakable sounds of Tilda and some man.

It had terrified Lily the first time Tilda had brought a man into the room. Lily had lain there, eyes squeezed shut, listening in horror. After he'd gone, that first time, Tilda had come and knelt by Lily's mattress. 'I'm sorry, Lily,' she'd whispered. 'But I've got to earn me money.'

The following day, they'd rigged a curtain up across the room, so as to give a little privacy to them both. Lily reminded herself that it was better than sleeping in a shop doorway.

★ ★ ★

'News, sir!' Arthur Bateman yelled, running up the gangplank onto the *Jenny Lyn*.

Jude was just emerging from below deck. 'What is it, Arthur?'

'News, sir! Good news!'

'That's what I like to hear,' said Jude. 'What is it, a new order?'

Ted waved a scrap of paper in the air. 'Not business, sir. I checked in at the newspaper offices — you'd asked me to, remember?'

'I remember,' Jude murmured, the strangest unsettling feeling stirring as all thoughts of shipping deserted him in a flash.

Arthur handed him the note. Jude saw two names and two addresses. Seeing the words *Lily Baines* made his head swim. 'This is where she's working?'

'Hope she's not working there, sir. That's not the most respectable street, so I'm told. Possibly she's lodging there. But I'm told that Lily Baines knocked on *this* woman's door only three days ago.'

Jude read the other name and a Bayswater address. He frowned. 'Why would Lily be knocking on a Mrs Rowen's door?'

'No idea, sir. This is all the information I've got.'

Jude needed to get there. Thoughts tumbled through his head, and a wave of emotion swept over him. He desperately needed to find this address. 'Thank you, Arthur. Thank you! There will be a few extra shillings in your pay packet this week. Can you get me a carriage?'

'I'm sure I can, sir,' Arthur answered with a grin.

Jude broke into a run, his heart racing. 'Don't worry, I'll get my own. Stay here and see that all remains well.'

* * *

Another day of door-knocking had finally paid off for Lily. A house in a quiet little cul-de-sac in Knightsbridge had a position vacant for a scullery maid. She had an interview lined up for the following day. She practically danced back home.

She paid little attention to the horse-drawn carriage standing at the kerb. For the first time in ages she felt positive and hopeful. She ran up the stone steps just as a man emerged through the door. They practically collided, and she would have toppled backwards had he not caught her arm.

'Whoops-a-daisy!' he said, steadying her. He seemed in no hurry to release her. Instead, his eyes glinted. 'My, but you're a pretty little thing. I don't suppose . . . '

'No!' Lily said, stopping him right there and then. 'I'm not that sort of girl.'

'Well, that's a real shame,' he said, still holding her.

'Not for me, it isn't,' Lily assured him pleasantly, happy that her luck could be changing. A decent job and place to live was finally on the horizon.

The man's grimy hands were still on her. 'You've got a lovely smile; anyone ever told you that?'

Her good mood plus a compliment made Lily's day. 'Thank you; now, if you — '

'Lily!'

A voice she thought she would never hear again resounded in her ears. She spun round. Jude Mitchell was standing on the pavement, his expression like thunder.

The grimy man was still hanging on to her. 'On yer bike, I was here first. Get yerself to the back of the queue.'

Jude lunged. Leaping up the steps, he grabbed the man by his jacket and hauled him down into the gutter. The carriage horses stamped their feet uneasily.

Lily gasped. 'Stop it!'

Jude, fists clenched, breathing hard, glowered down at the man. A second later, the fellow scrambled to his feet and ran.

The shock of seeing Jude was too much for Lily. An incredible wave of joy swept over her, followed instantly by a flood of anger. She couldn't think straight. Didn't know what to say, how to react. So, instead, she focused on the fact that he had just thrown a perfectly harmless man into the gutter for no apparent reason.

'You had no right to do that!' she cried, her heart pounding mercilessly.

He was breathing just as hard as her. 'You are quite right, Lily Baines, I had no right. But by God it felt good.'

'Have you lost your senses?'

'Possibly,' he uttered, staring at her like he couldn't actually believe his eyes. Looking her up and down with a look of disgust. 'So this is it? Your new line of work?'

In her confused state of mind, Lily was thinking of the scullery maid's job, and wondering why he should look so angry at that. Besides, she was the one who ought to be angry.

'And why not? I have to earn my own living . . . '

He staggered, as if her words had knocked him for six. Then his eyes turned glacial. 'Clearly you are a resounding success!'

'And clearly you're behaving like a madman,' Lily said, raising her voice, feeling suddenly like a street girl fighting out on the pavement.

'So I'm a madman, am I?' Jude uttered. 'And why wouldn't I be after finding you walking the streets, picking up men, selling your body?'

It was all so ludicrous that a bubble of hysterical laughter escaped her lips. 'What?'

'Did you have a wealthier client in Bayswater the other day?'

'What?' she uttered in disbelief. The man had lost his senses. 'You think . . . you think I'm a working girl?'

'If that's what it's called.'

Lily suddenly felt so enraged, and so protective of the women like Tilda, Aggie and Ruthie, who hadn't the good fortune in life to be cosseted and spoiled like Prudence but who had taken her in, given her a roof over her head and food in her belly.

'And what of you?' she argued back. 'What are you doing here in a notorious area? If I'm selling my body, you're obviously in the market for buying.'

His eyes narrowed. 'Not a chance.'

'So you were just passing, were you?'

'Actually, no. I was looking for you.'

She staggered. 'Why?'

A whole mixture of expressions flashed across his face; and then, as if not able to settle on any, he ran his fingers raggedly through his hair and said, 'Why indeed?'

Lily couldn't bear this. Bad enough he had lost her a home with the Westfalls, but now he was adding insult to injury. Angrily, she ran back up the steps, desperate to slam the door on him.

He caught her arm. 'Lily, wait!'

His touch was like fire. 'Let go of me!'

'Lily, get your things.'

She rocked on her heels, terrified he was about to say he owned this property and she was being thrown out. 'Pardon?'

'You live here, don't you?'

'I've nowhere else to go.' She felt nauseous. 'You want me to sleep on the streets?'

His blue eyes creased in pain. 'Why would I want that? I'm telling you to get your belongings because you're

261

coming with me.'

'I'm going nowhere with you!' she cried, tired of being pushed around. Pulling free, she ran indoors. She heard a sound of disapproval as the smell of damp and mildew hit him. Lily didn't even notice it these days.

'Lily!'

Fumbling with the door handle to her room, she burst in, Jude on her tail. They both stopped in their tracks. Tilda was in bed with a man. He took one look at Jude and leapt out, scrabbling for his trousers and boots, to make a run for the door.

Jude was swifter. He slammed it shut and leant against it, looking directly at Tilda. 'Does he owe you money?'

She shook her head, her eyes wide and a bemused smile on her face. Jude moved aside and allowed the man to escape. Then, without a word, he opened Lily's trunk and threw in everything he guessed was hers. 'Is that everything?'

Lily nodded, too shocked by the turn

of events to protest. Then, closing the catches on the trunk, Jude lifted it effortlessly and strode from the room. Over his shoulder he said, 'Say your goodbyes, Lily. I'll meet you outside.'

Tilda grabbed her nightdress and pulled it over her head before diving at Lily. Her eyes were huge. 'Who is that?'

Lost for words, Lily stood speechless. Finally, she managed, 'He's just . . . just someone I know.'

Tilda's smile widened. 'Well, you hang on to him, Lily Baines. You hang on good and tight.'

In a daze, Lily hugged Tilda, glad to be able to say goodbye and thank-you to one friend at least.

Stepping outside, Jude and the hackney carriage driver were busy securing her trunk. She felt drained, as if she had no control over her life. Forever being pushed from pillar to post.

Jude opened the carriage door. 'Get in, Lily.'

She hesitated. Reminded of when Ted

263

Draper had sent her away from everything and everyone she had ever known. Ruefully, she realised that history was repeating itself.

But again, she had no choice. If she refused, he might just drive off with all her possessions. Silently, she climbed into the carriage. It was stuffy and dark, and when Jude got in and closed the door, Lily had the sensation of being suffocated.

He was too close, sitting directly opposite her, his legs spread apart in this confined space, straddling hers as she sat with her knees tightly together, hands clasped in her lap.

Jude was staring at her. She wanted to stare back, to demand an apology for destroying her life. But her heart was beating too frantically, and she felt that to speak or argue might just result in her dissolving into tears.

They sat in a tortured silence, her thoughts tumbling over each other. He'd been looking for her. Perhaps he had put things right with the Westfalls.

Perhaps he was taking her back home to them.

The carriage rattled on through the streets and down towards the River Thames. She glimpsed the tall red-brick buildings alongside the waterfront. Saw a sign saying *The Port of London*, and remembered Jude had a fleet of cargo ships. Prudence had talked so much about how wealthy he was. They drove along by the river. Maybe he was going to throw her and her possessions into the Thames. He certainly looked bleak enough to do so.

'Do you plan on drowning me?' she found herself asking.

'Myself, more like.'

She had no idea what he meant by that. It wasn't him who had lost his home and everything he'd ever known. She stared through the carriage window as they travelled away from the docks, and eventually clattered down a neat and quiet road, lined either side by smart three-storied white-walled houses with not an urchin in sight. The carriage drew to a halt.

'Why have we stopped here?'

'My home,' he said abruptly, stepping from the carriage; then, as an after-thought, holding out his hand to assist her.

Lily ignored it, angry at him, angry with herself for not having the courage to have sent him packing and stayed with Tilda. But the last two weeks had sapped her energy.

So this was his large house in Whitechapel, as she recalled Lady Hester telling Prudence. Lily sighed. It was all bay windows and polished brass. Prudence would have loved this.

Jude carried her trunk into his house like it weighed no more than a basket of apples.

Reluctantly, Lily followed him in. The smell of beeswax polish instantly reminded her of Westfall Manor, and a wave of homesickness swept over her. She missed Mrs Pritchard and Sir Joseph so much. She even missed Prudence's flighty, self-centred ways.

'Go through and make yourself . . . at home,' Jude said, indicating a sitting room just off the hallway. 'I'll take your trunk upstairs.'

His tone was so clipped it was as if he despised her. His attitude was infuriating. Her predicament was all his doing. But she was too weary and hungry to argue.

Left alone, Lily gazed around the elegant sitting room. She guessed that many of the ornaments, rugs and paintings had come from the countries he'd travelled to. Yet there was a feminine touch to it, and she remembered he'd said his mother lived there too.

Minutes later, Jude was back. He stood, arms folded, scowling at her.

'Why am I here?' she asked.

'You preferred it where you were?'

'Actually, yes!' Lily retorted, her eyes flashing angrily.

He remained by the door, clearly not wanting to come anywhere near her. 'I gather you ran away to London to live that sort of life out of revenge? Because you saw Prudence kissing me?'

'What?' Lily breathed, not believing her ears. 'Ran away? You think I ran away?'

''Upped and left', was Hester's terminology. I admit, I thought she was lying. But I find it hard to believe she would have packed you off to a brothel.'

'Hester didn't care where I went,' Lily said, barely able to control her anger. 'But don't you dare look down your nose at those women. Maybe they haven't got two brass farthings to rub together, but they took me in, gave me a roof over my head, and shared their food with me.'

He fell silent for a moment, and then, his voice raw, he asked, 'And did you . . . did you share their way of life these last two weeks? Were you sleeping with men while I've been frantically searching for you?'

Lily clutched the back of an armchair for support as the room swam. His question tore her in half. Had he so badly misjudged her character as to think she would do that? Yet he'd been searching for her — why? Because he cared, as he'd said all along? She couldn't bear this. Being pushed and pulled in all directions. She really couldn't take much more . . .

She felt her body sway and her knees buckle.

'Lily!'

His voice sounded so far away, and the room with its many paintings spun crazily around and around. Strong arms caught her before she hit the floor.

She came to, to find herself lying on a sofa, Jude's blue eyes were level with hers, and she saw he was on his knees, dabbing her head with a cold flannel. For a moment, all that mattered was that Jude was here, beside her.

'You fainted. Are you ill?'

The pleasure of him being close vanished as she sensed his disapproval over her state of health. She struggled to sit up. 'I haven't caught anything contagious, if that's what's bothering you.'

'Lie still,' he instructed. 'And I wasn't implying that you'd caught some disease. I'm just concerned that you fainted.'

'It's hardly surprising!' she retorted. 'My life has been a trifle traumatic and exhausting these last few weeks. Perhaps you weren't aware of that. Being thrown out of my home, walking the streets, knocking on doors to try and find work so I didn't have to live in a brothel. You dragging me here before I'd had a bite to eat since early morning. That might account for me fainting.' She hoped her sardonic little speech wasn't lost on him, because now she felt totally exhausted.

'You haven't eaten today?'

She cast him a weary look.

He slapped his palm against his forehead. 'I'm such a fool. I'll get you something. Stay there, don't move.'

Despite still feeling light headed, Lily's hopes rose a little as she recalled

270

what he'd said just before she blacked out. *Frantically looking for her!*

He returned with a pot of tea and a bowl of potato-and-leek soup with bread and butter. He sat and watched her eat. It tasted divine.

'Feeling better?'

'Much better,' she admitted, as he put the dishes aside and sat next to her.

He was quiet for a moment, and then asked, 'Lily, tell me what happened. You didn't say goodbye to anyone. Not even a note.'

There was no animosity in his face now. Lily saw that he was prepared to listen. Taking a deep breath, she told him the full story. He listened without interrupting, except for the occasional utterance of anger or sympathy. Finally, she asked, 'Was Sir Joseph angry, thinking I'd just left without a word?'

'Not angry,' said Jude, seeming to choose his words carefully. 'He was very upset. The kitchen staff were too.'

'I need to write to them. But I imagine Lady Hester will intercept my letters. She won't want people knowing she sent me away.'

'Especially her husband! And I shall personally make sure he does know.' Jude took her hand in his, sending Lily's heart fluttering. 'Lily, I am so sorry for what happened. My behaviour was appalling. No wonder Hester wanted rid of you. She could see I was falling in love with you.'

With all her heart, Lily wished she could believe him. 'Yet you kissed Prudence, so soon after telling me how much you cared.'

'I swear to you, Lily, I made no advances on her. I was trying to let her down kindly, and she misconstrued my words. But that evening, when Hester announced that you'd gone — my world fell apart.'

'Did it?' Lily murmured. 'I thought — I really thought it was Prudence you wanted.'

'Never! I searched for a note, stupidly thinking you might have left me a forwarding address.'

'I never returned from Ted Draper's farm . . . '

He squeezed her hands. 'I know that now. But then I was bereft to find your room stripped bare; there was no trace of you. You'd vanished into thin air — as did all my hopes and dreams.'

Her heart swelled with love. 'Well, I am here now, Jude. And if you truly want me, I will stay.'

He held her, softly murmuring, 'This is where you belong, my darling. Right here in my arms.'

14

Jude prepared a hot bath for Lily, and reluctantly left her to soak and wash away the grime of London's streets. Now alone in his room, he tried not to imagine her sitting naked in his bathtub. These last few hours had been emotional turmoil. Sheer bliss to find Lily again. Then hell to find her living with prostitutes. He had stopped thinking rationally then, and instead acted like a complete fool. His assumptions must have been the worst thing he could have said, particularly when it had been his fault for removing her from a decent home — with her father, though she hadn't known it, her half-sister and stepmother.

It was unbelievable that Hester had got rid of her so cruelly.

He needed to speak to Sir Joseph. For one thing, to let him know Lily was safe and with him. Also to urge Sir Joseph to tell Lily the truth, that he was her father. And, most importantly, to ask for her hand in marriage.

* * *

The hot water made Lily's cheeks glow. She glowed inwardly too. Jude had admitted he was falling in love with her. And there was to be no marriage between him and Prudence. She could not have felt happier.

He had prepared a room for her, and Lily sank into the feather-filled bedding with a blissful sigh. She was asleep within seconds. When she finally awoke, it was late morning.

Butterflies danced in her stomach as she went downstairs, and it came as a pleasant surprise to meet Jude's mother in the dining room. They were so alike. The same intense blue eyes and strong bone structure, but while he was tall and broad-shouldered, his mother was petite.

Her face lit up on seeing Lily, and she kissed her on both cheeks. 'Lily, hello! I'm Adele. How lovely to meet you at last. My son has told me what a dreadful time you've had of late.'

Wryly, Lily wondered if he'd told her it was mostly his fault.

She ushered Lily to the dining table and poured her a cup of tea. 'What would you like for breakfast, dear? Could you eat poached eggs on toast?'

'I would love that!' Lily all but drooled.

'Well, relax and drink your tea while I get that ready for you.'

'Can I help?'

'By all means, another day. But as you're a guest, I'm more than happy to cook your breakfast.'

It surprised Lily that Jude's mother did her own cooking. She couldn't imagine Hester standing at the hob or washing pots. 'Thank you. I used to cook at Westfall Manor.'

'Yes, Jude told me. And he told me about that dreadful woman who forced

276

you to leave without a moment's notice. What a spiteful thing to do!'

'She had her reasons,' Lily murmured. For all her harshness, she couldn't forget that Lady Hester had provided a home and education for her these last eighteen years.

'No doubt. But selfish reasons, I expect.' Adele didn't wait for a response, but added, 'My dear, let me have the address of those street girls who were so kind to you. I might be able to help them . . .'

Jude came in looking very handsome in beige breeches and black shirt. 'My mother belongs to a welfare society helping the disadvantaged.'

Lily's heart lurched upon seeing him again. 'That's very admirable.'

'It keeps me busy,' Adele remarked cheerfully. 'You know what they say about idle hands.'

Her remark reminded Lily of Mrs Pritchard, and in turn her job interview today. 'Oh! I've just remembered, I have an interview today as a scullery maid.'

Jude's dark eyebrows joined in a frown. 'Lily, you don't need a job, you can stay here . . . '

She stopped him right there. 'Jude, all my life I've been living under someone's roof out of the kindness of their hearts; but I need to support myself, work for a living, earn a wage and pay my way. I need to know where I belong.'

'I'll see to breakfast while you talk,' said Adele, smiling approvingly at Lily as she left the room.

Jude's expression mirrored his mother's. 'That's admirable, Lily, but you could do much better than being a scullery maid.'

'It's an honest job. My mother was a scullery maid.'

'Yes, it's a very respectable job, but there are other trades you could consider.'

'Jude, it's not easy finding employment. I have blisters on my feet to prove that.'

'Have you?' He sounded concerned,

and looked as if he wanted to cradle her feet in his hands and soothe away the soreness. 'Lily. I admire your tenacity, but I'm here now.'

'Yes And I'm grateful to you and your mother for your hospitality . . . '

'I don't want gratitude, Lily. In fact, I'd like you to consider a different proposition.'

Her eyes widened, wary of what he was about to suggest. But under no circumstances would she accept charity or be beholden to anyone ever again.

He crossed to the window and gazed out. 'As you know, I have a fleet of merchant sailing ships.'

'Yes?' She was puzzled.

He turned to face her. 'What I would like — and what I'd be willing to pay for, on a weekly basis — would be for you to work as an illustrator for my company.'

She had been sipping tea. Now the cup clattered onto her saucer. 'An illustrator?'

'I've seen your artwork, Lily. I know

how meticulous and talented you are.' His expression became animated, as if his thoughts were falling into place only seconds before voicing them. 'I often advertise in the newspapers. Just think how attractive my advertisements would be if they were illustrated, and my letter-headings too.'

He was offering her a dream job, presumably out of guilt. Before she could speak, however, he came and sat beside her. 'And before you give me some high-and-mighty reason to refuse, Lily, I must tell you that I have always longed to have some oil paintings done of my ships. My father and grandfather built up this fleet. How I would love to have paintings hanging on these walls.'

She was glad she was sitting down. 'Oh, my word!'

'What do you say, Lily?' He grasped her hand. 'Isn't that better than raking out ashes and peeling potatoes?'

'There's nothing wrong with . . .'

He silenced her with a kiss. It was so sudden, so unexpected, that she simply closed her eyes and floated off to paradise.

'You have a rare talent, Lily,' he murmured. 'It would be criminal not to use it.'

She tried to speak — to act as if a million stars had not just exploded in her head. 'The idea is very appealing, but I have to find lodgings; that job came with its own room.'

'Lily, you have a home here.'

She shook her head. 'No doubt you feel responsible for my homelessness, but I've been beholden to people all my life . . . '

'Then pay for your room if it makes you feel better: I'll deduct ten percent of your wages for rent.'

She was lost to know what to do, and he was starting to look exasperated. 'You're just being kind.'

'In which case, I'll take twenty percent of your wages — no . . . ' His voice became dangerously husky. 'I'll take ninety percent . . . and as many of those sweet kisses whenever I like.'

His arms encircled her, his kiss urgent. Lily felt the fire rage inside her body, every nerve tingling with longing for him. The sound of the door handle turning brought them back to their senses.

'Breakfast!' announced Adele, and a fresh pot of coffee.'

As they ate, Jude explained his proposal to his mother, who thought it a perfect idea.

'In fact, Lily, the society I'm with could make good use of your artistic skills too. An artist could draw the people and the conditions they are living in. I swear it's the only way to make the government act to help the poor of London.'

'There!' Jude said, rubbing his hands together. 'You are very much in demand. But I would like Lily to work with me to begin with. Perhaps, when I sail, you pair could put some sort of report together which could be published.' He looked hopefully at her. 'That's if you want to, Lily.'

Convinced that they weren't just being charitable towards her, she exclaimed, 'I would love to!'

'Wonderful!' cried Adele. 'You'll be a marvellous asset to us, Lily.'

Jude breathed a contented sigh. 'Lily Baines, you have no idea how happy you have made me.'

If he was half as happy as she was, he would be delirious. But as she ate her breakfast she worried that if this bubble of happiness was to burst now, she really didn't know how she would survive.

Once breakfast was over, Jude was keen to show Lily his fleet and his workplace. Armed with sketchpad and pencils, they walked to the docks. On the way Jude talked enthusiastically about his ships and the places they sailed to. Lily listened rapturously, loving the sound of his voice and fascinated by his stories.

They came at last to tall iron gates bearing the name of St Katharine's Docks, and beyond them Lily stared in wonder at the sight of hundreds of tall ships' masts, furled sails and huge brick warehouses seven or eight storeys high. Out on the grey choppy waters were dozens of rowing boats, ferrying back and forth to the large ships anchored out in the estuary.

'Oh, Jude! I've never seen such a sight!'

'Take my arm, Lily,' Jude said, threading her hand through the crook of his elbow.

The clamour and commotion was incredible as workmen and sailors shouted to one another and barrels, crates and sacks full of goodness knew what were unloaded from the ships, rattling and clanking down gangplanks. Trolleys trundled over cobblestones while hoists and pulleys hauled heavy loads up into warehouses.

'It's wonderful! I can't wait to start sketching.'

He laughed. 'Wonderful is hardly the word I would use to describe it! But it would be wonderful to see the world through your eyes, Lily.'

'Thank you,' she murmured, eager to capture the scene on paper. 'Could I sit somewhere and draw?'

'Not *just* here,' he said, sidestepping her out of the path of a mule and cart piled with bulging hessian sacks smelling of coffee. The man leading the mule nodded at Jude, who nodded back. 'Good man. Keep your wits about you as they weigh it.'

'Yes, Mr Mitchell,' the man answered, urging the mule forward.

Jude explained the procedure to Lily. 'Imports have to be weighed and measured and a tax levied at the Custom and Excise office here. Then it's taxed depending on what it is and where it's going on to.'

'I see.' Lily nodded, fascinated by all the activity and content in knowing that he valued her. She truly felt she was where she belonged — by his side.

Fascinated, she watched goods being lifted up on a hoist, and saw how the men leant right out of the building to drag the cargo into the warehouse.

'As you can see, Lily, it's dangerous work.'

He led the way into a warehouse where crates, barrels and sacks full of all kinds of commodities were stored. Jude took great pride in pointing out the coffee, tea, tobacco and spices, explaining where each had come from and where it would now be distributed.

He led the way up an echoing stone stairway to the fourth floor and into an office. It was a pleasant room, quite warm because of a small stove where a kettle was steaming merrily away.

'My office,' he said, resting his hand on a worn and cracked leather chair next to a mahogany desk. 'And my father's and grandfather's before me.'

She wandered to the window and gazed out. 'I'd like to draw this view. It's very dramatic.'

He stood directly behind her and, to her delight, slid his arms around her waist. She leant back against him, her heart overflowing with love and happiness.

'You know, Lily, I'm due to leave in a few days time for a month-long voyage to Europe on the *Jenny Lyn*.'

It was a magnificent sailing ship, but her happiness ebbed a little. She hid her feelings. 'It must be very exciting, seeing the world.'

'One port looks much like the next. I'll be more excited coming back home . . . '

Behind them, someone coughed politely. Jude released her and Lily saw a wiry-looking man holding a wad of paperwork. His smile stretched from ear to ear.

'Lily, this is Arthur Bateman, my right-hand man. Arthur, this is Lily Baines, the young lady your detective work helped to locate.'

'I can hardly take credit, but I'm delighted you found her, sir.' He whispered to Lily, 'Like a bear with a sore head, he was. Good job we weren't out to sea, or he'd have had us all walking the plank.'

Lily laughed, delighted to hear that Jude had missed her. 'How did you find me, anyway?'

'Mr Mitchell put an advertisement in the paper,' Arthur explained. 'Asking if anyone knew of your whereabouts. A Mrs Rowen in Bayswater contacted us.'

Lily recalled the woman who had so carefully noted her address. It must have been her. 'Thank you for doing that,' she said shyly, her eyes locked onto Jude's.

He looked as if he wanted to hold her, but instead he wheeled his leather chair to the window. 'Arthur, Lily is to be our official illustrator. Our fleet will be immortalised in oils.'

'What excellent news!'

'She's to be on our payroll. I'll give you the details later.'

'Glad to have you aboard, miss. And right glad to have Mr Mitchell back — the proper Mr Mitchell.'

Jude led Lily to his chair. 'Well, we have work to do. Lily, will you be all right to stay here and sketch while I carry on? Make tea for yourself; you'll even find biscuits if you look hard enough.'

'I'm perfectly fine here,' Lily assured him. 'But later, could I get a closer look at a ship? Maybe even go on board?'

The two men exchanged glances. 'Generally people can't wait to get off!' said Jude. 'But if that's what your heart desires . . . For now we'll leave you to your work.'

Work! Lily loved the notion of working for a living. Oh, if only she could tell Mrs Pritchard. She would write at the first opportunity, and hope her letter got through. She would tell her that she was safe and . . . happy.

A glow spread through her body. Yes, she was happy — deliriously happy. Jude cared for her and she was now a working artist. How incredible that fate could so quickly turn despair into joy.

But then a small dark cloud drifted by, warning her that fate could just as easily turn the tables back again.

15

On board the *Jenny Lyn*, Jude tried to keep his mind on the job in hand. He and his foreman checked the ship over from stern to hull, but his mind constantly strayed. He couldn't believe his good fortune that Lily was back in his life. And that she cared for him. Oh, the way she responded to his kiss and his touch! He could only dream of how she would respond to him in bed. The thought sent his pulse racing and blood throbbing through his veins.

The prospect of the month-long voyage coming up troubled him, leaving Lily so soon after finding her. Particularly as he had not fully committed to her yet — to ask her to be his wife. But he needed to speak to Sir Joseph first. To get his blessing. Time was of the essence.

'Arthur,' Jude said, clasping his

foreman's shoulder, 'I need to travel to Sussex again. Can I leave all the final preparations for our voyage in your capable hands?'

'Of course, sir.'

'Good man.' Jude stood on deck, his hair blowing in the breeze, eyes fixed on that fourth-floor window where Lily sat.

Arthur Bateman followed his gaze. 'Sir, if you wanted to stay home for this trip, I can captain the *Jenny Lyn*. I've done it before, as you well know.'

Jude sighed. 'Thank you, Arthur, but I will be back in time to set sail. Have no fear.'

'It's your choice, sir.'

'Indeed,' agreed Jude with a sigh. 'Indeed it is.'

★　★　★

Lily had done page after page of sketches and written notes about colours, lighting and shadows to help her when she was working in oils back home . . . *home*. Could she think of it as home? Dared she?

In one of her sketches of the *Jenny Lyn* she had included Jude. He had looked so majestic standing on deck, legs apart, looking so buccaneer. She watched him then, striding down the gangplank with his foreman almost running to keep up. There was nothing about him that she didn't love. And when he returned to his office she had to refrain from running into his arms. He seemed breathless and his eyes swept over her, as if drinking in the sight of her. But she was being fanciful. He was no doubt breathless from climbing four flights of stairs, not because of her.

'Did you manage to sketch anything?' he asked.

'Oh, yes. But they're just rough drawings.'

'Can I see?'

She felt shy suddenly. This wasn't her best work. There were just so many things to look at.

'They're not very good yet.'

'You're too modest,' he said, closing the door and taking the sketchpad from her. 'May I see?'

'It's all a bit of a jumble, but back home . . . ' She stopped, embarrassed.

'Yes, Lily, you can call it home.' He smiled, making her heart leap. And then turned the pages, studying her work.

She felt compelled to move closer, to point out her own failings. 'It's not too impressive at the moment. For instance, that building is quite out of proportion, and that mule looks like a dog with rabbit's ears, and . . . '

To her astonishment, he planted a kiss on her lips, silencing her. 'I understand! These are rough drafts; and you, Lily Baines, have the sweetest lips which I could kiss forever and ever.'

He put her sketchpad aside, his arms sliding around her waist, moulding her to his hard torso. She could feel his heart beating in time with her own. 'How I've ached for you, Lily! The sleepless nights you've put me through.'

She slid her arms around his neck, raising her face to receive more of his kisses. 'I'm here now, Jude,' she murmured against his lips.

'Yes, thank God. You are.'

Lily would have happily stayed in his arms for the entire afternoon, but he had things to do. Finally, holding her at arm's length, he sighed reluctantly.

'Put your shawl on again, Lily, and I'll take you on board the *Jenny Lyn*.'

'You will!' She could barely contain her excitement. With sketchpad and pencils, she followed him willingly down the stairs and out onto the quayside.

He led the way, keeping her close, one hand at the small of her back, guarding and guiding her between carts and barrows and men who stopped to stare.

'Lily, when I'm away at sea, please never come here alone. It wouldn't be safe. While I know my own crew, I can't vouch for every Tom, Dick and Harry. I'd be happier knowing you were at home perfecting your artwork. Or with my mother making sketches of the slum areas of the city.'

She made her promise, and boarded the *Jenny Lyn*, marvelling at the size of it. It was sturdy and his crew greeted him with respect. The fluid sensation of being on a ship was strange but Lily could well imagine the thrill of casting off from the quayside, the ship's sails being unfurled and billowing in the wind as they set out towards the high seas.

'It must be so exciting heading off to foreign shores,' she said wistfully.

'Would you like to see the world, Lily?'

She gazed into his face, realising that her one true desire was simply to be close to him. She almost said, *only if you were with me*, but her courage deserted her and she replied, 'I would love to.'

'Perhaps we will arrange for you to accompany me on a voyage, one day.'

Her heart soared. 'Oh! Yes, please.

That would be wonderful!'

He laughed at her enthusiasm. 'The prospect of seasickness wouldn't put you off, then?'

'My goodness, no. I'm sure that would pass in no time.'

'I love your confidence, Lily. Seasickness was your . . . your friend Prudence's main concern.'

Lily's heart plummeted. So he had already asked Prudence to accompany him on a voyage. She turned away on the pretence of taking in a different view. All her initial instincts were back with a vengeance. Prudence — her. Comparing one with another. Deciding which was the better catch.

Jude followed her and stared down into the grey water. 'Lily, there are places where the ocean is the colour of your eyes, and coral as pink as your cheeks. Places where you can see below the depths to another world.'

She couldn't look at him. She had read in Sir Joseph's books of the ocean being blue. It was Prudence's eyes which were blue; hers were violet. And Prudence's cheeks were pink. She was pale. Clearly his words were a practised line simply to impress. Her heart felt like a lead weight in her breast.

'Jude, I think I've seen enough. And . . . and it's quite chilly out here on the water.'

'Are you all right, Lily? You look very pale suddenly.'

'I'm always pale.' She bit back the urge to remind him it was Prudence who had rosy cheeks.

His frown deepened. 'I've upset you in some way.'

'Not at all!' she lied, turning sharply away, hoping to reach the gangplank in some sort of dignified manner. Gripping the rail, she tottered unsteadily down the steep wooden ramp.

He came after her. 'Lily, why are you running away from me?'

'I'm not!'

'So if I was to take you in my arms and kiss your now, would you respond as you did earlier, or would you push me away?'

She felt the heat rise up her throat and into her cheeks. Her face would certainly be rosy now. 'I trust you would not embarrass me in such a manner!'

His gaze burned through her, and then he sighed. 'No, Lily. I would not embarrass you. But I would sincerely like to know what I've said to send you scuttling behind that iron façade again.'

Lily swallowed hard, feeling foolish and jealous. 'Could we talk somewhere a little more private? I think we're amusing the entire workforce of Saint Katharine's Docks standing here.'

'Indeed,' he agreed, taking her elbow and escorting her towards the gates.

She walked in stony silence, but regrets swamped her. They were leaving, and there were still so many scenes she wanted to sketch, but her own foolishness and insecurities had spoiled everything.

Back onto the cobbled streets of

London, Jude led the way, not suggesting she linked her hand into his arm, not once glancing her way. Streets widened and shops lined both sides of the road. Well-to-do people browsed shop windows, and Lily could imagine Lady Hester and Prudence being quite at home here.

Jude startled her by suddenly taking her arm and weaving between the horse-drawn carriages to the other side of the road. A small church stood behind iron railings. Jude pushed open the gate and led her through.

'I don't know if this will interest you. But this is my family's church. I was baptised here, my parents married here, and I married Isabella here.' His gaze focused into the distance. 'It's also the last resting place of my ancestors — as well as my father and my wife.'

Her heart lurched. Sensing his pain, she touched his hand. 'Oh, Jude!'

His fingers closed around hers. 'Please don't shut me out, Lily. Tell me what I said that made you so angry with me.'

Her jealousy seemed so insignificant suddenly. The fact was, he had brought *her* here to such an important place — not Prudence. She hung her head. 'I was being foolish. I didn't mean to shut you out.'

There was pain in his eyes. 'I hope not, because you have a place in my heart where I want you to stay forever.'

Her happiness soared once more, and the world with all its commotion and passers-by ceased to exist as Jude took her in his arms and kissed her.

It was the disapproving tut-tutting of one such passer-by that had them laughing like children and walking back onto the street.

Arm in arm, they strolled along the pavements. Eventually Jude stopped outside an art shop. The pebbled bay windows were festooned with art materials.

'Let's look inside,' he suggested, pushing open the door.

There was the smell of oils and paints, and the shelves were stocked with sketchpads, canvases, brushes, pencils and paints. The shopkeeper in his embroidered waistcoat was as colourful as his shop.

After surveying the shelves, Jude said, 'We'll need an easel, a palette, oil paints, new brushes, and some large canvases.' He glanced at Lily. 'What else will you need?'

'My goodness!'

His eyebrows rose. 'Well, you'll need these materials if you're to do the job properly, Lily.'

He was clearly taking her role as his company's illustrator seriously. And so she browsed further and added a few more items to the list, which Jude arranged to be delivered to his address. The shop owner was practically bowing and scraping by the time they left.

'You're so generous, Jude. I hope I can do all this justice.'

'I know you will do your best, and that's all I ask.' He threaded her arm through his, holding her close. 'And this afternoon, I shall clear one of the bedrooms so you have space to work.'

'Could I help you do that?'

His face lit up. 'I would like that very much, Lily.'

*　*　*

The next two days passed in a whirlwind of activity. Jude created a studio for her facing east, so she would have the sun in the mornings. She accompanied him on more visits to the docks, and her sketchpad was soon crammed full of ideas. Another of his ships, *The Golden Rose*, set sail, and she stood with Jude at the furthest point of the docks to witness its huge sails billowing in the wind as it sailed up the estuary to begin its voyage. Lily sketched rapidly, moving to catch it from different angles. When it was little more than a dot in the distance, Jude slipped his arm around her shoulders.

'I'm looking forward to seeing that in oils, Lily.'

'I can't wait to start work on it . . . '

There was a sadness in his voice suddenly. 'Three more days, and I set sail on the *Jenny Lyn*. I'll be away a month, maybe more.'

She rested her head against his chest. 'I'll be here when you return.'

He sighed. 'And before that, I have other business to attend to. I'll be away tomorrow and may not get back until the following day. It's important, or I would not be wasting my last days away from you.'

A tiny shudder ran through her body. *Last days?* She pushed the ominous little thought out of her mind and refused to let passing comments spoil her happiness.

16

Lying in bed, knowing Lily was so close, was torturous. Jude desperately wanted to make love to her, and it took every scrap of willpower not to give in to his desires. So far she had not spoken of loving him, but the way she responded to his embraces and kisses seemed to say she had feelings for him. He prayed he wasn't mistaken.

Tomorrow he would travel back to Westfall Manor and give Sir Joseph the good news that Lily was safe with him. He only hoped Sir Joseph would give him his blessing for a marriage. That was, if Lily would have him. No doubt Hester and Prudence would not take the news well.

Jude awoke as dawn was breaking. He washed and dressed quickly, eager to be ready when his carriage came. Passing Lily's bedroom door, he hesitated. God, how he longed to slip between the sheets and feel her warm softness close to him.

He heaved a sigh. He had to be patient. Nevertheless, he peeped around the door to gaze briefly at the woman he loved. She was sleeping soundly, her long silky hair splayed across the pillow, lashes resting softly on her cheeks. He hoped she was dreaming of him.

He had time for coffee and toast before the two-horsed carriage arrived. Before climbing in he warned the driver about the potholed lane on the approach to Westfall Manor. This time there would not be a beautiful young woman racing to his rescue.

The journey seemed endless, but it gave him time to think and make plans. Eventually, Jude alighted, paid the driver and made arrangements for the return journey. He guessed Sir Joseph would give him a bed for the night, but if Lady Hester showed him the door, he would walk to the village and find a room at the coaching inn.

The young maid answered his knocking. Seeing him, her face lit up.

'Hello, Dorothy. Is Sir Joseph at home?'

She bobbed a curtsey. 'I believe so, Mr Mitchell. Please come in.'

His boots echoed hollowly on the tiled floor. The house felt like an empty shell, knowing Lily was not here. He couldn't wait to be back with her.

Still smiling at him, Dorothy checked the library and study before reporting back. 'He might be out on the estate; he's been spending a lot of time away from the manor recently. I'll find Lady Hester.'

She tapped the dining-room door and went in. Jude heard his name mentioned, and a moment later Prudence came dashing out. 'Is Lily with you?'

Jude bowed his head. 'Good day, Prudence. Forgive the intrusion, I was hoping to speak to Sir Joseph.'

Lady Hester appeared then, as stiff

and upright as a wooden stake. Her expression was sour. 'Mr Mitchell, this is unexpected. What business do you have with my husband?'

'It's a personal matter, my lady.'

Her face pinched even more. 'I have no idea where he is. Out, possibly.'

He bowed again. 'Then I'll go and find him. Perhaps, if he returns in the meantime, you'd be kind enough to tell him I'm here and would like a word of a most important nature?'

'Have you news of Lily?' Prudence begged, clasping her hands together.

If he wasn't mistaken, Prudence lacked her usual sparkle. 'Lily is well . . .'

'Oh, thank goodness!' Prudence gasped, turning to look at her mother.

Jude held back his anger. 'Ladies, I'm well aware that Lily did not leave of her own accord.'

Prudence hung her head shamefully. Hester did the opposite and tilted her chin.

'The address you sent her to,' Jude

continued, 'had long since changed ownership. The house is now a brothel.'

'A brothel! How apt!' dismissed Hester.

Prudence gasped. 'Mama, you said you'd spoken to Mrs Caldwell. You said Lily was to be a cook for her!'

Hester shrugged one stiff shoulder. 'How was I to know?'

'Poor Lily! Mama, we have to bring her home. I miss her so much!'

'She stole your husband-to-be, just like her mother stole my husband!' Hester snapped.

Prudence blushed. 'Jude and I were never betrothed . . . '

'You never had the chance!'

Sir Joseph emerged from upstairs. He looked thinner, and pale. 'What's going on . . . Jude. Jude, do you have news of Lily?'

Prudence ran and clutched her father's arm. 'Papa, I'm so sorry. Mama and I sent Lily away . . . '

'Silence!' Hester raged. 'Prudence, I forbid you to speak another word.'

'I have to, Mama.' She looked ashamedly at her father. 'I . . . I was jealous, because Jude seemed so interested in Lily; and Mama was furious, because she wanted him to propose to me. She thought he would never do so with Lily around, so we packed her off, and we lied about it. We said she'd gone of her own accord.'

The older man staggered. Prudence clutched his hand. 'I'm sorry, Papa. Mama sent her to a house in London.'

Sir Joseph stared at his wife and daughter in disbelief. 'You've had an address for Lily all this time?'

Prudence began to cry. 'I'm sorry. Do you hate me? I can't blame you . . . '

Hester turned aside, her stiff frock rustling. 'I'm not listening to another word.'

Sir Joseph cupped Prudence's chin. 'Prudence, what you did was wrong, but I understand. And I think it's time I told you something about Lily . . . '

'We're sisters, aren't we? Well, half-sisters. You're her father.'

His mouth dropped. 'Your mother told you?'

She shook her head. 'No. I guessed because of how sad you've been. And she has your looks — well, she's much prettier than you, but . . .'

He smiled, and then the sombre look was back. 'I betrayed my wife by falling in love with Lily's mother, so we brushed the fact that Lily was my child under the carpet.'

Prudence's face lit up. 'But surely we can bring her home now, can't we, Papa?'

'Yes, most definitely.'

Jude cleared his throat. 'Sir, actually, there is something I need to ask you.'

Sir Joseph and Prudence looked at him.

'You may or may not believe in love at first sight, but that's how I feel towards Lily. I would, sir, if you'll give us your blessing, like to take Lily's hand in marriage.'

He'd expected Prudence to go into a sulk, but to his surprise she squealed in delight. 'I'll be her maid of honour! Jude, please can I?'

Jude raised his eyebrows in surprise at her attitude. 'I would dearly like your father's blessing first, and then I think it will depend on Lily.'

Sir Joseph's eyes closed for a moment, taking it all in. Jude waited, scarcely breathing, Prudence almost bouncing with excitement. Finally, Sir Joseph took in a deep breath. 'I can't think of anything better for my Lily. You are a good man, and I know you will take care of her. Better than I have done these last eighteen years.'

'Oh, Papa!' Prudence cried, hugging him. 'You've been trying not to hurt Mama. You're the best father in the world.'

'I'm glad you think so, Prudence. But not everyone would say so.'

'I don't care what anyone else says,' Prudence exclaimed. 'You're wonderful. And Lily is so lucky. Actually, she's doubly lucky — Jude loves her too!'

Sir Joseph came and shook Jude's

hand, and then wrapped his arms around him. 'I'm happy for you. Happy for you both. But how will Lily react to knowing I'm her father? She might never forgive me for keeping it secret.'

'Well, sir, the best person to give her that news would be yourself,' said Jude, his heart swelling with happiness.

'We must make arrangements. Jude, will you stay the night, so we might have a chance to talk? How did you manage to find her, and is she well? We must arrange when I can visit her.'

'Me too, Papa,' Prudence squealed. 'Lily and I can go shopping together. London has some wonderful shops. Oh, I can't wait to tell Mrs Pritchard!' She dashed off towards the kitchen, shouting, 'Mrs Pritchard, Dorothy, you'll never guess . . . '

Sir Joseph clasped Jude's hand again. 'I am indebted to you, Jude.'

At dinner, later that evening, Hester listened to what everyone had to say without a word. Only at the end of the meal did she announce that she would be visiting her cousin the following morning and wouldn't be back until late.

'I think she's too embarrassed to face me,' Sir Joseph whispered as she swept out of the room.

Jude sighed. 'I hope all this has not put your own marriage in jeopardy.'

Sir Joseph's eyebrows arched. 'We live quite separate lives anyway. My fault, of course. But things will never improve unless she forgives me. Eighteen years have passed, and she still hasn't. I don't see things changing very much in the future.'

'That's very unfortunate,' Jude said.

Sir Joseph looked him straight in the eye. 'Be sure that you marry Lily, then, Jude. Don't let her slip out of your fingers. Don't live a life of regret.'

'Sir, I value your advice. The moment I return home, I shall ask Lily if she will be my wife. And I swear I will love and cherish her forever.'

That night, he slept soundly. Happy in the knowledge that finally all was well.

17

Placing a pristine canvas on her easel, Lily began mixing paints on her palette. The sun was shining through the windows of her room — her *studio*, as Jude had named it — and she felt overwhelmed with happiness.

The one black cloud on the horizon was the prospect of Jude sailing tomorrow. She longed for him to return from his business trip so they could share some time together before he had to set sail.

A little later, the sound of someone knocking the front door startled her. Wiping her hands on a cloth, she ran down the stairs. Adele had gone out an hour ago on her charity work, and it wouldn't be Jude unless he'd forgotten his key, which wasn't likely. Possibly it was another delivery from the art shop. She opened the door, and her smile vanished.

'Lady Hester!'

Standing primly on her doorstep in a dark grey bonnet and shawl, Hester's face was as pinched as if there was a bad smell under her nose. 'Lily. I see Mrs Caldwell's home was not up to scratch, hence you've wormed your way into Mr Mitchell's household.'

Lily stood there, lost for words.

'Were you brought up to leave visitors standing on the doorstep?'

'No, please come in,' Lily uttered, standing back as Lady Hester brushed past her. She made her way into the sitting room and stood taking stock.

'Landed on your feet yet again?'

Lily let the remark go, determined not to be intimidated. 'This is a surprise, Lady Hester. What brings you to London? I'm afraid Jude . . . Mr Mitchell is away on business at the moment, and his mother is out.'

Hester settled into Jude's chair as if she owned it. 'I know only too well where Jude Mitchell is at this moment, but it's you I've come to see.'

'You know where Jude is?' Lily puzzled. 'But how?'

'Because right now he is at the manor.'

That surprised Lily for a moment, then she guessed he had gone to reassure Sir Joseph and Mrs Pritchard that she was safe.

'I see. And your reason to see me?' Lily asked, wondering if Hester had come to apologise. Somehow she doubted it.

Hester smiled. It was an unpleasant smile. 'I've come bearing news for you, Lily. I thought it time you knew your background . . . knew who your father is.'

A tremor ran through Lily's body. 'You know?'

'Of course I know!' She eyed her coldly. 'I've always known who your mother had a sordid little affair with that culminated in you being born!'

'It wasn't a sordid affair!' Lily cried, touching the cross around her neck.

Hester's voice rose. 'Sleeping with a married man *is* a sordid affair!'

Lily's heart sank. So he was married. That explained so much. 'You can't help who you fall in love with.'

'Oh, I think you can, if you've any decency about you.'

Hester was wrong, but perhaps she'd never experienced true love. There was no point arguing about it. Lily took a steadying breath. 'And will you tell me who my father is?'

For what seemed an eternity Hester remained silent, and then two words burst from her mouth like venom.

'My husband!'

Lily felt as if she'd been slapped in the face, then slumped down onto a chair. 'Sir Joseph! How . . . how long have you known?'

'Eighteen years. Of course, he hadn't the courage to tell me. It was just so obvious. The way he held your mother as she lay dying. The way he cradled you in his arms.' She turned her head aside. 'It made me sick!'

Lily could barely speak. 'Why didn't you send me to an orphanage?'

Hester's eyes narrowed. 'That would have been too easy. I wanted him to suffer. I wanted him to watch you growing up, a constant reminder of his infidelity. And you've grown up just like her. Not just in looks, but in the way you stole Jude from under Prudence's nose.'

'Jude was never attracted to Prudence.'

'Well, of course you'd say that!'

'Does Prudence know that we are half-sisters?'

'Of course — and Jude Mitchell. And you're wrong about him not being attracted to Prudence. Why do you think he's at the manor right now?'

It shocked Lily to hear that Jude knew but had never said. 'How long has Jude known I'm Sir Joseph's daughter?'

Hester was enjoying this. 'The evening of your sudden departure. The fuss my husband made when I told him you'd upped and left. But you should have seen the way Jude Mitchell's eyes lit up.'

Lily wanted to call the woman's bluff. Jude couldn't have known she was Sir Joseph's daughter. He would have told her, surely.

'My husband was desperate to find you. He begged Jude Mitchell to search for you. I imagine he paid him handsomely to trace you. And probably to look after you should he find you.'

Lily's head was beginning to throb. She stumbled to her feet. 'Thank you for telling me. I'll bid you good day now.'

'I haven't quite finished,' said Hester, rising to her feet. 'As I said, Jude Mitchell is at this moment with Prudence. I believe the man has marriage in mind. I believe he is trying to make sure he is making the right choice as to which daughter to wed. After all, you will both be very wealthy women in time. And marrying into money is important to Jude Mitchell, that's quite obvious.'

319

Lily's heart was breaking. She wanted desperately to shout at this vindictive woman that she was wrong about Jude, but the truth was, Hester was most probably right.

Head high, Hester strolled to the door. 'I've told Prudence to turn him down should he propose. But you know Prudence, a handsome face turns the silly girl's head. Don't be surprised if he proposes to you once she's said no. I'll bid you good day.'

Trembling from head to toe, Lily closed the door on her. Slowly, she walked back into the sitting room, sank down onto the sofa, and wept.

* * *

It was early evening when Lily heard Jude's key turn in the lock. She checked her reflection, glad to see there was no evidence of her misery. Her eyes were no longer red and puffy. She'd even managed to begin a few pencilled outlines on her canvas. She heard him

320

call her name from the hallway. She ignored it, concentrating on mixing two blue paints together on her palette. But her heart thudded as he ran up the stairs two at a time.

He came straight in and swept her up into his arms, his mouth on hers, kissing her like a starving man. Despite everything, despite Hester giving her such dreadful news, Lily couldn't stop her innermost emotions overriding her good sense; and she kissed him and held him tight, while inside her heart shattered into a thousand pieces.

He had been paid to find her. He knew she was Sir Joseph's daughter. He had been to see Prudence. Somehow she kept the tears at bay.

Holding her at arm's length, his face radiated happiness. She almost asked him if Prudence had turned him down, and whether it had made his decision easier. Either way, he would be getting a woman with some wealth behind her.

'Lily, are you all right?' His smiled faded a little. 'You're very pale.'

She put on a smile. 'I'm perfectly well. How was your trip?'

'Wonderful. I'm sorry I'm so late back, but there was something I had to get from the city.'

'So, your trip went to plan.'

'Exactly to plan!' he said, kissing her again.

She wanted to tell him not to kiss her, but the truth was, she loved him. She tried to think straight. Perhaps she should have taken no notice of what Hester had said. She could just have been causing trouble. Despite herself, she asked casually, 'Where . . . where did you go?'

He took her hand, leading her downstairs. 'All in good time. I believe Adele has made dinner and I'm starved. Shall we go down?'

Food was the last thing on her mind, but she put on a smile. Adele served dinner, eager to share some news.

'Lily, I met the dear girl who took you in — Tilda.'

'Really? How is she?' Lily asked,

trying to match her enthusiasm.

'Well, in dire need of direction, but quite robust and in good spirits. She was pleased to hear that you have a nice home now, and work.'

'I'm glad she's well.'

'We had a long chat, and I've offered her and another of the women a job working at one of the mills. I have contacts. It's hard work, but they would earn a fair wage. Enough to cover their rent and food without resorting to what they do now.'

For a moment, Lily forgot her own troubles. 'Thank you for doing that, Adele.'

They talked all through dinner, and after coffee Adele informed them that she would be out early in the morning and not back till late. She bade them goodnight, but Jude followed her out of the room, saying there was something he needed to talk to her about.

Lily had the feeling it was something to do with his visit to Westfall Manor. For all she knew, he could be planning on bringing Prudence here to live as his wife, and keeping Lily on as an employee.

Returning, Jude sat beside her and took her hands in his. 'Lily, there's something I want to ask you.'

'Go ahead,' she said, a little sharply. Whatever it was, she sensed it was something important. It angered her that whatever it was, he'd left it until almost the last moment before setting sail, leaving her to cope with whatever news he was about to impart.

Then he frowned. 'Lily, I sense the barrier is back up. Please tell me I'm wrong.'

She felt as stiff as Lady Hester. 'What is it you need to ask me?'

His gaze flicked over her face, but then the smile was back. He took something from his inside pocket, and then, to her astonishment, went down on one knee. He lifted the lid of the box. 'Lily Baines, I've loved you since I first set eyes on you. Would you please do me the greatest honour of becoming my wife?'

She swayed in shock. Nestled on a cushion of red velvet was the most beautiful gold ring glittering with rubies and diamonds. Her heart soared, but then Hester's words came flooding back: *Don't be surprised if he proposes to you once she's said no.*

Lily couldn't speak. Everything Hester had predicted had come true. The pain was too great. She spoke without thinking. 'So, Prudence turned you down, did she?'

His happiness seemed to crumble into dust. 'Prudence?'

'You've been to Westfall Manor. Please don't deny it, Jude.'

'I'm not about to deny it.'

'And you saw Prudence?'

'I had no choice but to see Prudence.'

Her eyes fluttered shut for a moment. 'And you made your choice as to which daughter was the better catch!'

'Lily!' He looked as if she'd dealt him a mortal blow. He got to his feet, still holding the ring.

Lily jumped to her feet too, hurt beyond words. She'd been right about this man all along. 'You knew I was Sir Joseph's daughter! You knew and you didn't tell me!'

'Yes, I knew, but it was down to him to tell you, not me. That's why I visited him. To tell him you were safe with me and to ask him for your hand in marriage.'

'How much did he pay you to find me?'

He rocked on his heels. For a long-drawn-out moment he just stared at her. And then he clicked the ring box shut. 'He didn't pay me a damn farthing. What on earth put that idea in your head?'

'Did you propose to Prudence today? Did she turn you down? Should that ring be on her finger right now?'

'After all I've said to you!' He sounded mortally wounded. 'You still have no trust in me. No matter what I say or do, you don't trust me. So perhaps I *should* have proposed to

Prudence. Perhaps I don't cope well with complicated women. I've told you that I love you, Lily. I've told you that I want to marry you. I can't do any more. I think the decision you've just made is the best one for the both of us. I'll bid you goodnight!'

He stormed from the room, and from the house.

For the second time that day, Lily sat and wept.

* * *

She couldn't sleep. She lay tossing and turning, going over and over the events of the day and of the past few weeks. She loved Jude; she had from the moment she set eyes on him. But she'd fought it all the way. Now, according to Hester, he'd only come looking for her because Sir Joseph, her *father*, had paid him to do so. But what if that was a lie? What if that was Hester being vindictive?

Even if it were true, that her father

had paid Jude to try and find her, was she so proud as to turn him down? Forego the chance of happiness, of *belonging*, just because of her own pride? Wasn't it possible that he might be attracted to two women? Did she really think she was so special that he *had* to choose her? She wasn't special. She had never been special.

But he was. She loved him dearly, even if he was guilty of being seduced by the thought of two wealthy daughters to choose from.

She couldn't bear this. She couldn't bear her thoughts swirling round and round in her head. She couldn't bear feeling this wretched. And she couldn't bear to think that maybe she had just broken Jude's heart.

Although it was the middle of the night, she got up, pulled on a gown, and went softly along the corridor to his bedroom. She needed him. To talk. To be in his arms. She needed him so badly.

She crept into his room. The curtains were open. Moonlight shone across his empty bed.

18

The following morning, the house was empty. Adele had gone out. Jude hadn't returned. And today was the day he set sail for a month-long voyage. Lily's thoughts were in turmoil. Should she try and find her way to the dock, to try and speak to him? But would he want to speak to her? She doubted it. But to have him leave without a word . . . It was unbearable.

Perhaps he would be back. Surely he would have to pack. Lily paced the room, looking out the window every few minutes. And then, when she was in the kitchen, a knock came at the door.

Lily's first instinct was that Hester was back to make more mischief. Unless it was Jude. He'd stormed out without his key. He was back! She ran to the door and threw it wide.

Sir Joseph and Prudence stood there,

anxiety etched on their faces. Lily gripped the door frame to steady herself.

'Lily!' Sir Joseph uttered her name.

'Father!' The word left her lips so easily, so naturally. And tears welled up into his eyes. Lily took his hands, drawing him into the house, her eyes searching his face.

'Forgive me, Lily. Forgive me for these last eighteen years.'

'There's nothing to forgive.' She led him into the sitting room, and sat close to him on the settee. Prudence stood awkwardly, a handkerchief clutched in her hands. Lily reached up and took her hand, drawing her down beside her too.

'I'm sorry too, Lily. I'm so stupid, letting Mama send you away, and to such a horrible place.'

'It's over and done with.'

Sir Joseph touched the cross around her throat. 'You're still wearing it.'

'I'll wear it forever.'

'I thought you'd be wearing another piece of jewellery by now!' said

Prudence, pointing to Lily's left hand.

'Shusshh!' Sir Joseph halted her. 'Jude may not have . . . you know.'

Lily looked at their faces. It surprised her that Prudence was being so amiable. She hadn't boasted that she'd turned Jude down. In fact, she seemed to be trying to contain her excitement.

'Well, has he?'

'What?'

'You know! Proposed?'

Taken aback, Lily answered, 'Well, actually he has . . . '

'You lucky, lucky thing!' Prudence squealed. 'Oh, I'm not jealous — well, all right, I am a bit green — but honestly, Lily, I'm so happy and excited for you. When Jude turned up at our house yesterday he was so excited about asking Papa for your hand in marriage. Oh, how romantic! I truly wasn't too jealous.'

'So . . . he didn't ask you first?' Lily found herself asking.

Prudence giggled, not taking the

remark seriously at all. 'I wish! No, honestly. You and he are so right for each other. And I'm so happy because he's going to be my brother-in-law anyway.' Her blue eyes sparkled. 'We're sisters, you know — well, half-sisters. Isn't that wonderful!'

Lily nodded, her eyes welling up with tears.

Sir Joseph wrapped his arms around her. 'Oh, Lily, the times I have wanted to hold you. When you were little and you'd fallen over and hurt yourself. It broke my heart not to be able to hug you, and soothe your fears and pains. I'd promised *her*, though — Hester. I owed it to her.'

'I understand, Father.' It was wonderful and unbelievable to be able to call him that, even though her heart was aching over Jude. 'Hester was here yesterday.'

Sir Joseph was taken aback. 'Was she? She told us she was visiting her cousin.'

'Well, she came here, and I think it was to make mischief.'

'In what way?' Sir Joseph asked kindly.

Lily explained what Hester had said, and how it had impacted on Jude.

'I didn't pay Jude to find you!' Sir Joseph said in astonishment. 'I would happily have given away a fortune if it could have brought you back. But there was no need. Jude loves you, Lily. He was so happy yesterday when he came to ask for your hand in marriage. He loves you, my darling daughter. He loves you with his whole heart.'

'Then I've spoiled everything,' Lily breathed. 'There's to be no marriage, and he sets sail for a month-long voyage today.'

'Papa! We have to do something!' Prudence cried, clutching Lily's hand.

'My carriage is outside. If we hurry . . . '

'Quickly, Lily!'

Lily snatched her shawl, and the three hurried from the house and into the waiting carriage.

'Saint Katharine's Docks, quick as

you can!' Sir Joseph ordered.

Rattling along at a speed that made Prudence squeal in excitement, they reached the docks in record time. Lily clambered out and ran. All the smells and commotion she remembered from being here with Jude just days ago engulfed her. She ran along the cobbled quayside, dodging the mule carts and the sailors and crewmen.

And then she saw the empty space where the *Jenny Lyn* had been anchored, and her heart dropped.

She stopped one of the workers. 'The *Jenny Lyn*, has it been moved?'

'You could say that,' the man answered looking off into the distance. 'She set sail ten minutes ago. That's her in the distance.'

A bleak void of desolation swept over her. Silently, she walked to the furthest point of the quay, and watched Jude's ship until it was gone.

Her father and Prudence were standing by the carriage.

'We were too late,' Lily murmured,

trying to smile. Trying to pretend that her heart wasn't broken.

Her father held her while Prudence assured her that he'd soon be back, and that a month was no time at all.

'I think I'll just go for a walk, on my own,' Lily said, giving them her key from her purse. 'Please, go back to my house, make yourself at home. Adele will be home later. You'll like her.'

She didn't wait for them to agree or disagree. She set off, walking blindly, not caring where she was headed. This was all her own fault. She should have trusted in Jude, not listened to Hester's spitefulness. Well, the woman had had her revenge now. She'd halted any romance between her and Jude. She'd succeeded.

Lily lost track of time or direction, and it was only when she spotted a familiar little church that she realised where she'd ended up. Jude's family church. Wistfully, she guessed that if she'd said yes to Jude, this was where they would have married.

Eyes downcast, she wandered between the gravestones. One or two people were tending graves. One person who had been kneelin, got to his feet. Something about him caught Lily's eye. His height, the broadness of his shoulders, the long leather boots; the way he stood, legs astride, as if balancing on a ship on a stormy sea.

Her heart flipped. And then she ran. Hitching up her skirt, she wove her way through the headstones. 'Jude!'

He spun round, and his tear-stained sorrowful face suddenly lit up in a look of disbelief and joy. He strode towards her, and without a word swept her up into his arm, raining kisses and tears onto her lips, her face, her eyes, her throat.

'My Lily!' he sobbed.

'You didn't sail!'

'I couldn't leave you! I've been standing here, looking for divine inspiration as to how I was ever going to make you love me and trust me.'

'I do love you, Jude. I love you so

much. But I was a fool. Hester came to see me yesterday; she lied and I listened and believed her, rather than trusting you. I'm so sorry!'

'That dreadful woman . . . '

'I came looking for you. I went to your room last night . . . '

'Did you?' He gazed at her, and then slowly the sparkle came back into his eyes. He smiled. That wonderful smile of his. 'I was at the docks all night, making last-minute preparations for my foreman to captain the *Jenny Lyn*. I knew I'd never be able to leave you.'

'I thought you'd gone. My heart broke.'

His eyes shone wickedly. 'So you went to my room — what would you have done, if you'd found me in bed?'

Tingling with happiness and desire, her hands stroked his face. 'I would have slipped under the covers beside you, and shown you how much I love you . . . '

It was all she had the chance to say. His lips claimed hers, and not even the tut-tutting of a passer-by could separate them.

Then, taking her hand, they walked to the front of the church. Taking a small box from his pocket, he went down on one knee. 'My darling Lily Baines, I love you with my heart and soul. Please do me the honour of becoming my wife.'

Her heart soared with joy. 'Oh, Jude, yes! Yes! Yes!'

He stood, kissed her, and slipped the ring onto her finger. Out on the street, a small crowd of passers-by who had stopped to watch gave a rousing cheer.

Laughing, Jude dragged her into the cool of the church. 'So we'll set the date ... soon, because I don't have the willpower to wait another hour! And then we'd better let your father and Prudence know. I think she wants to be your maid of honour and help you choose your wedding gown.'

'Jude, my darling. They're already here, at home.'

He held her lovingly. 'I like the way

you say *home*, Lily. *Our* home — where you belong.'

She raised her face to receive his kiss. '*This* is where I belong, Jude. In your arms.'

We do hope that you have enjoyed reading this large print book.

Did you know that all of our titles are available for purchase?

We publish a wide range of high quality large print books including:
Romances, Mysteries, Classics
General Fiction
Non Fiction and Westerns

Special interest titles available in large print are:
The Little Oxford Dictionary
Music Book, Song Book
Hymn Book, Service Book

Also available from us courtesy of Oxford University Press:
Young Readers' Dictionary
(large print edition)
Young Readers' Thesaurus
(large print edition)

For further information or a free brochure, please contact us at:
Ulverscroft Large Print Books Ltd.,
The Green, Bradgate Road, Anstey,
Leicester, LE7 7FU, England.
Tel: (00 44) **0116 236 4325**
Fax: (00 44) **0116 234 0205**

PAWS FOR LOVE

Sarah Purdue

Sam rescues animals and trains assistance dogs — but has less understanding of people! Meanwhile, Henry is desperate to help his young son Toby, who hasn't spoken since his mother died. Toby's therapist has suggested that an assistance dog might help the boy. Unfortunately, Henry Wakefield is terrified of dogs! But when Sam brings Juno into their lives, Toby begins to blossom and Henry starts to relax. Will Juno prove to be a large and hairy Cupid for Sam and Henry?

ALWAYS THE BRIDESMAID

Jo Bartlett

Finally moving home after five years in Australia waiting in vain for faithless Josh, Olivia is welcomed back into the heart of her best friend's family on the Kent coast. Cakes, donkeys, weddings and a fulfilling summer job — all is wonderful, except for her unsettling attraction to Seth, who is moving to the United States after the summer. Is it worth taking a chance on love, or would it just lead to more heartbreak?

CORA'S CHRISTMAS KISS

Alison May

Cora and Liam have both experienced horrible years that have led them to the same unlikely place — spending December working in the grotto at Golding's department store. Under the cover of a Father Christmas fat suit and an extremely unflattering reindeer costume, they find comfort in sharing their tales of woe during their bleak staffroom lunch breaks. But is their new-found friendship just for Christmas? Or have they created something deeper, something that could carry them through to a hopeful new year?

CHRISTMAS AT THE LITTLE VILLAGE SCHOOL

Jane Lovering

Working at a tiny village school in rural Yorkshire has its own unique set of challenges — but when Lydia Knight and Jake Immingham are tasked with getting the children to put on a Christmas play for the local elderly people's home, they know they're in for a tricky term! From choreographing sugar plum dance routines to dealing with reindeer costume malfunctions, Lydia realises that, even as a teacher, she isn't past being taught a couple of things — and one of those things is a much-needed lesson in Christmas spirit.